Into The FIre

Settling The Sangre's, Volume 2

D.C.Ludlow

Published by D.C.Ludlow, 2024.

This is a work of fiction. Similarities to real people, places, or events are entirely coincidental.

INTO THE FIRE

First edition. February 6, 2024.

Copyright © 2024 D.C.Ludlow.

ISBN: 979-8224996049

Written by D.C.Ludlow.

Settling the Sangre's
Book 2
Into the Fire

Ok. So... Where were we that last time you guys came to visit? Oh yeah. The time I got caught alone on the wrong side of the mountains. I had been captured and I had to escape from the Indians. That was in Northern Wyoming that time.

SO let me back up a little bit for a moment so I can get the story straight and then I'll continue.

My partners Tom Sweet, Paul McVeigh and I have been working in the Rocky Mountains for a couple of years now and have done quite well indeed. The first season I did well enough to outfit my own party of trappers and hunters and move into fresh territory. While the crew was doing well with their jobs in the rivers, streams and lakes of the mountains, I went on a scouting trip into deeper country. What I found there was a rich, untapped new trapping grounds for the next season. My men and I would once again spend the winter in search of better places to trap beaver.

I also found there a people I have never encountered before, and had almost lost my life in the venture. Though I was lucky to escape the Indians with my life, I was injured in a fall and had to spend weeks in a cave to rehabilitate well enough to rejoin my men. I was saved by a very strange man who lived in the cave; alone for years in the wilds of a savage land. He called himself Father Levetti, and claimed to be a Catholic priest with a calling to minister and save the people inhabiting this region of the mountains; the Crow.

It was the Crow who had taken me captive and from which whomI had to run for my life and escape a truly gruesome fate. I did not fully believe this so called priest, and upon further investigation into this cave home of his I had found what looked like a weapons and supplies cache left over from when the Spanish had invaded and occupied this region decades before. In looking over the cache of supplies I came across a map, and though it was in Spanish and I couldn't read it, I instantly knew the value of a map of the region to the south; A a place called the Sangre De Cristo Mountains that stretched down into Mexican Territory, and a place the Mexicans even referred to with respect and fear. A place known as The Comancheria, or Comanche land.

From what I had heard about these roving bands of Comanche and Kiowa further west, I truly hoped I would never have to fight them. They were, by reputation, the fiercest and most brutal of the tribes. Even the Cheyenne and Sioux who had fought them over territory and hunting grounds for ages had a great respect for their warriors' fighting ability. It was rumored in the camps at rendezvous that a Comanche on his horse was the perfect plains warrior, and one to be feared!

Now that I have rejoined my men and am healing well from this misadventure, I have new priorities to consider. For one, we have lost two men to a mountain lion attack, Michael McNeil and Abe Hatfield. I am responsible for this, as they trusted me with their lives on this adventure and in that respect I have failed them. When we get to rendezvous and sell our furs, David must be paid his brother's share and seen on his way. Secondly, Abe's family must be contacted and given his share of the season' reaping. Until then, it must be business as usual. The wilderness does not wait for injuries to fully recover, and many times being convalescent can be deadly!

Next is to figure the key to reading this map I found, and possibly find my way to the places marked there and find out what they mean. For all I know they are markers of the graves of fallen soldiers. Or maybe they are the places where some great battle took place, or the location of the Indian tribes' major encampments. In any even I believe this map will be instrumental in finding new lands to explore and see what is there!

So as I continue my story, I will begin where I left off last time you were here. But I will warn you, the story is not always pleasant, as life was not always pleasant. I had no idea what situation I would lead my men into next, and in truth, there were many times I feared for our lives, and did not think we would survive it!

Chapter 1

Now that the mountains were mostly covered in snow, my men and I had to work in the lower valleys with their ponds and streams. There were plenty of good places to trap still, they were just harder to get to and from the trap lines. Snow drifts built up with the winds, and storms that seemed to come one after another. We spent most of our time holed up in camp keeping fires going and waiting out the worst of the storms. We also now had to be on constant watch for Indian raiders, even through the winter.

I had no idea if the Crow knew of the cave, the lions den, that went trough from this side of the mountains to the other. Until this side was completely blocked by the snow I could not relax security for the camp. Instead of splitting back up into two man groups, we all stayed in two camps staged a couple hundred yards apart, hidden in the lower tree line along the valley floor. On alternating days some would go north and check trap lines some would go south. Always leaving us with a strength of men in camp to defend it if necessary.

On days that were sunny, we divided forces and some would check traps and others would hunt. We always had a great need for fresh game, and most were quite adept at bringing meat to camp. It was decided by a common vote I was not privy to, that I should remain in camp and heal completely before I returned to any further ventures into new territory. I believe more so the men just wanted me to stay in camp in order to be protected from any further possibility of losing their contact to greater prices for our pelts come rendezvous. In either case I did not argue the point as I too agreed I needed to regather my strength before anything more finished me off completely.

Although this system was working well, I soon began to become restless in camp and began to take on much of the hunting duties myself. Long Walker and I scouted for enemies and whatever game we could find. Those injured in the lions den had healed quite well by now as well. All but David's state of mind. He remained sullen and angry. He preferred to work alone as much as he could. The loss of his brother had hit him hard and he was not recovering from it well at all.

I remember one day, after a particularly hard day for us all, We had all gathered in one camp to discuss plans for the coming weeks. This was the day before we were to move the camps to new areas, as we were starting to come short in the traps in out current location. We had an elk roast on the spit over the fire and Tom was putting together some of his biscuits with the last of the flour.

It was just before sunset and the rays became golden but tinted the horizon in an array of pinks and oranges against the baby blue of the sky. The land was covered in snow that reflected the colors of the skies, giving the effect of it being a painting done with colors I had never seen before. The horses stood three legged at the picket line where they too would benefit from the heat of the fire.

Some of the men smoked their pipes, while others looked to the repair and maintenance of the traps and other gear. As always Saul and Cole were cleaning their rifles when Cole brought up a decent proposal. "How about we check out that canyon up north a ways, over that saddle under that set of pointed peaks there." He pointed while he spoke at a region we had not investigated before. "Me and Saul was about to go there ourselves before we had to go find you."

"Likely spot?" I asked "You get to scout it out good?"

He nodded and went on "We counted 12 dams on one stream alone and there are 3 streams there that we found." Saul broke in "Plenty of tracks as well, coyote, bobcat, saw some wolf, elk, deer, antelope and bear as well as the tell tale beaver sign along the streams."

"Much Indian sign?" Samuel asked "Where there's plenty of game there's plenty of Indians!" Cole replied with a shrug "Not so's you'd notice. No more than anywhere else." Samuel pit his pipe and responded through the cloud, "Don't mean there ain't none there!" Cole nodded and had to admit "True enough I s'pose."

Then David spoke up sarcastically "Well we all knows what ta do with the bloody bastards now don't we? Take their hair before they take ours, I say!"

A couple of the men nodded in agreement but no one spoke to his comment "How far ya reckon it is from here" I asked. "Cant be more than maybe 20 mile id say." Saul said while scratching his beard. "But I don't think even that far." "Well fellas, what say you?" I asked. We had agreed at the beginning of the season that we all had a say in major decisions effecting everyone. "I'm game if yer takin' a vote" Sam spoke up first. "I am."I nodded. The rest one by one gave their "Aye!" til it came to Long Walker. "Well Saul and Cole already spoke their vote by suggestin' it, so how about you Long?" I asked.

"Oh now yer giving a vote to a Indian?" David interrupted, "As if that don't beat all!" He stormed off, shaking his head, to relieve himself behind a tree. "I go where you and Tom go," Was the Utes simple reply. "Then it is settled" I announced "We'll follow your lead come morning after we break down the camps. Y'all got all the traps and pelts in already?" All agreed all supplies and gear had been collected up and ready to move. "All but two, that is" Samuel interjected "I forgot I had some good wolf sign on a set nearby, and I re-baited just in case they come again. Ill collect it up in the morning."

"Good enough." I nodded back to him. Cole changed the subject after by askin' "Hey Tom them biscuits done yet? My belly's startin' to think I got my throat cut here!" Tom shouted back "Yeah yeah! Hold yer water! They're bout done!"

As the men turned their attention to eating, the conversation shifted to what each thought to do with their share at rendezvous. "I wonder if Ol' One Legged Pete will show up with his whores this year." Cole mused. "You an' whores, Cole, I swear" Saul shook his head "You'll be the poorest man in camp in two days after cashin' in, if'n yer not careful!"

"Mebbe so, but I'll be the happiest about it too!" Cole shot back, "Cant spend it out here, and damn shore ain't gonna be able to take it with me when its my time!" Tom looked over the fire at Cole's rifle, an old Tennessee style flintlock with a stock repaired with a rawhide patch after it broke in a fight. "I'd think you'd be needin' to get a new rifle there Cole that old flint banger looks about used up!"

"It is true," Cole admitted, "But Ol' Dru here been with me a long time and I'd feel I was a cheatin' on her if'n I was to get a new rifle." Cole had named his rifle after an old sweetheart back in Missouri. "Mebbe I'll git me a couple o them new pistols though... that'd be nice. I seen one on traders row last year at rendezvous what had two barrels each on em! I heard of em before but never seen em."

Samuel spoke up next "I'm gonna buy some of those Appaloosa horses from up in the Northwest territory. Dick Cooper had himself a half a dozen in camp last year. Id like to have a couple of those. Good strong mountain horses they are!"

David scoffed and stood up, "I'd be careful if I was you, me lad, word I heard was he stole them horses off some chief up there.. them Nez Perce on the Powder River. I wouldn't wanna be dodgin' any more Indians than now would you?"

Samuel laughed outright at his cousin, "Stole em?? Id like to see the look on ol' Dicks face if you was to accuse him of stealin' horses! Especially from the Nez Perce. His wife is the daughter of one of their chiefs. He didn't steal them horses!"

Tom interjected here to change the subject. "How bout you Silas?" he asked me "You got any plans for your share after we resupply?" I just looked at him and Cole and winked "I might just go have a look at those horses myself! I'm gonna be doing a lotta scoutin' again next fall and a good mountain horse is gonna come in handy!" Tom just rolled his eyes "Not another scoutin' trip! Silas we talked about this!" He always knew how to make me laugh only laughing still hurt! "Just lookin' into a couple stories I heard Tom nothing to get excited about." I reassured him "Somethin' about that Levi that don't add up." I decided that was about all I should say just then.

"Oh so its a mystery then is it?" Samuel blurted, ever the true Scot he could never say anything quietly. "You might say that Sam," I agreed but again left my answer vague "But I wont know till I check it out now wouldn't ya say?" Samuel took my hint and let it drop. Little by little as the men finished eating the conversation died down as some smoked their pipes and passed the last of the whiskey. It wasn't long till most retired to their tents for the night, while those on first watch scouted the perimeter.

Tom and I usually were up later than most as we used this time to make plans or discuss things other than business. We kept the fire low so we could more easily see into the darkness, just enough to keep warm. At times it would be religion as I am a Protestant and Tom a devout Catholic. Other times it would be the philosophies of Plato or Socrates. Other evenings we discussed the plays of Shakespeare. Tonight though it was the mystery of the priest in a cave where he shouldn't be, and the odd contents of that cave.

"I cant say as he lied to me so much as maybe he dint tell me the whole truth. About him OR about those things in the cave." I kept my voice low so as to not be heard by anyone but Tom. Its not that I didn't trust my men but I wasn't sure of anything, and felt it best to not say too much to the others yet. "Why would a priest be hoarding up maps and mining tools. I KNOW those tools are newer than what the Spanish had! And rock samples.. I jus' dunno Tom. And who was the skeleton I found?"

Tom was always a good listener, "Well I can see what you mean by wantin' to go scoutin' more next season. But you know I gotta go in on that with ya! I'm not gonna go though what happened this season again!" I was hoping he would say that, of course, "I was thinkin' of havin' Paul with us this season and not running a different crew. He knows about mining and may be helpful to have along." I looked at him through the smoke of the fire and he was nodding.

"..you say so... I just met the man when he signed on. He ain't no Company Man but you know how some of them *Independent types* can be!" I could tell he was being sarcastic by now. So I went with it, "Yeah Yeah yeah, there's no tellin' what we might do!"

• • • •

DAVID MCNEIL QUIETLY poked a couple sticks into his fire and rolled over into his blankets to mull over the conversation he had just heard. He had a lot of thinking to do now, and plans of his own to be made by spring. To be sure HE knew what to do with information like this he had just overheard. All he need do now was to play along and let them lead him to his own little pot o gold! Mining equipment indeed!

Chapter 2

Whice Eyes awoke from his sleep to feel his breath bubble in his chest and rattle in his throat. He felt as though he had been running for half a day, but he had been asleep in his lodge. He struggled to sit up, and found his breath came easier as he did. He moved carefully to his sitting place by the fire and pulled his buffalo robe close over his shoulders. He could hear the even slow breaths of his wives as they slept. He reached out and found the pile of sticks for the fire where it always was, and took some to put into the dying coals of the fire.

He began to feel the heat on his face and hands as the coals caught and began to blaze up into a flame. He could hear the horses stamping and blowing in the distance. Farther off he heard the yipping of a lone coyote, probably calling to its mate. He heard the crickets of the night all around and all else was quiet, as it should be. Yet something did not feel right, as if he was in a dream. Was he sleeping and dreaming of being awake? No.. that could not be so.

The bubbling in his chest was causing him pain, and he began to cough. His head swam and spun with each cough. With a little effort and concentration he was able to control his breathing again, and spat up what he had coughed into the fire. He HAD been dreaming, as he was riding his red spotted horse, a horse that had been stolen in a raid by the Comanche half his lifetime ago; when he could still see.

As he remembered more of his dream, he saw that he had been riding through his homeland where his people camped in the long valley under the mountains. But he saw many strange things as he rode.

He saw white men crawling in and out of holes in the ground. So many he could not count them; their faces twisted with greed and hate. He saw many rows of the square lodges white men lived in where his people used to hunt buffalo.

The buffalo was now a scrawny and weakened beast with long straight horns and no winter coat. When he looked to the sky, he saw a giant bird that flew without flapping its wings, and had a cry like that of a great battle, loud enough to deafen his ears!

His breath began to feel even more ragged in his chest, but his eyes were wide with his vision. He saw a huge metal snake that moved on ribbons of shiny metal across the land. When the snake stopped white people would crawl from its belly and infest the land. His breath caught painfully in his lungs as he saw his people, crowded onto a small corner of a desert where there was no life. They were dying of hunger surrounded by blue men on horses.

His vision became so real to his blind eyes that he began to sing his death song, though he could only whisper. He watched the blue men and their guns kill hundreds of his people and their cousins while they slept. Men, women, children, old, sick; they cut them down with their long knives and hacked them to pieces for trophies. He felt a tear on his cheek as he watched the lodges of his people burn.

Out of the smoke of the fires he saw his children's children wandering, lost and starving. Their hair cut short and dressed in rags, trying to live a white mans life. Unhappy and sick, their spirits dead inside them, they walked but were more ghosts than people.

Now his breath was hard to draw, he struggled to get air to his lungs which bubbled as though filled with water. His chest became heavy as if his horse had rolled on him. His vision faded and he could no longer sing his death song. His voice now coming as a ragged whisper.

Pain gripped his heart and his head began to swim again. How was he laid on his back again? Was he not just sitting by his fire? He struggled to breathe and his body began to shudder with the effort. His hands clutched at the pain in his chest.

He looked down and he could see his body still twitching, his mouth agape but drawing no breath. Behind him he heard the voice of his grandfather and his father calling him. He turned to look and saw all the members of his people who had gone on before beckoning him to cross the blackness and join them.

He turned once more to look at his body laying in his lodge but there was only black there. What had he turned to see? Why was he looking behind him as his people were just over the river in front of him? How was it he could see again? He simply shrugged and rode his red spotted horse across the river and went home to the land of his people.

White eyes, Old one, father of Dull Knife and Young Elk, Chief of the People of the Big Beak Bird, was dead.

Chapter 3

Not every day was a good day in the mountains. We were constantly assaulted with bad weather and violent storms. The life of a trapper is not an easy one, but we were up to the task. After the incident with the lion in the cave most of the men felt a brotherhood that only living through danger can induce. The one exception to this was David.

David had become surly and confrontational, often going off to work alone, which was very dangerous in these wild places. The threat of death came from all directions, whether from the bears that freely roamed these mountains, or from the tribes of Indians that were unfriendly to whites in their lands.

One day while we were working a set of streams on the Weed River, we heard a shot just to the north of our position, up a little creek that David had decided to work alone that day. Just after there were a few more shots, which could only mean he was under attack. We caught up the horses and quickly mounted bareback and took off in the direction the shots were heard.

If David had just shot an animal for food or to take its fur, like a coyote or a wolf, there would have been only one shot, making it difficult to tell where it had come from. But with the ongoing sound of rifle fire we had a pretty good idea where to go.

By the time we got to the bend in the creek David had been working, we saw he was hunkered down in a good defensible spot among a set of fallen trees on the creek bank to use for cover. A couple hundred feet away there was a group of what looked like Blackfoot retreating into the trees as we approached. They obviously had seen us coming. This was good for David, as it gave him a moment to catch his breath from having to hold them off alone. In truth we didn't know how he had survived due to the fact that they held the high ground and, if not for the logs David crouched behind, he would most likely have been dead by the time we arrived.

It was only by chance that we came up from behind his position, and the Blackfoot retreated into the tree line. They could plainly see we had come to join the fight. Once we got to David's position the fight was on! The warriors took turns making runs at our position in order to try and flank us but we had a fine field of vision and could easily control the front of our position as well as the flank to the right as it was a thick copse of trees that even an Indian would have a hard time navigating quickly.

"Seems ya pissed em off David! I think they want your hair!" Cole was always the one to point out the obvious. "Yeah well, It isn't the first time!" David shouted back as he finished reloading his Hawken. The others all found suitable cover as quickly as they could before the Indians could regroup and charge.

"Who in the hell are these fellas??" Samuel asked "Any idea on how many there be?" while organizing his pistols in a row on the log for easy access during any further assault. "I have no idea now do I??" David cried "I just looked up and there they was a'comin towards me on the creep! I dunno who they are! I just shot one off for help and they charged me!! They didn't count on me havin 2 rifles and 2 pistols! That made em run!"

"Look like Blackfoot to me!" Tom shouted from his cover behind a boulder a few yards away. "Next time maybe don't shoot unless *they* do!!"

A war whoop came from the tree line, and we could see a lone warrior standing with raised war club, taunting us to break cover and attack. "Hold yer water boys, don't let em goad ya into a fight. Let em come!" I instructed. I took a sight on the warrior and held it there but held off the trigger. He was too far for an accurate shot just yet. Besides, this may yet have been merely a taunt before they would just leave the field. That fantasy was soon dashed.

All at once several more warriors charged out from the tree line all screaming bloody hell and ran right towards our position. "They're gonna flank us boys!" Tom shouted "This is a distraction!" Tom had fought Indians before and knew that a frontal assault like this was meant to keep us busy in front of us while the real threat snuck up on us.

I let out a slow long breath as the warrior I had sighted came closer. They might know how far a musket can shoot... or even a Hawken, but little did they know of Long Stick! I gently squeezed the trigger and the rifle bucked. All the while I kept my eyes on the man I had targeted until the thick white smoke of my powder obscured him from sight. When the smoke cleared, the man was down and not moving.

All these men knew how to fight. It was required in order to just survive in these mountains. Many were veterans of Indian conflicts all their lives. Sometimes fighting with the Indians as well as sometimes against them. This was very helpful in staying alive in this territory!

I ducked down as the other men began to fire and motioned to Tom and Long Walker to keep eyes on our flank and hold their fire in reserve. I peered through the thick smoke as I struggled to reload Long Stick. Having a much longer rifle than most men had, I found myself in too tight a spot to reload easily. Suddenly an arrow thudded into the log inches from my head, and I was forced to duck down almost flat in order to be out of sight.

"Here they come!" Samuel shouted and he fired his rifle at the same time as an arrow tore into the bicep of his left arm. He just began to reload as if he didn't notice. "How many are there?" Cole shouted to David. "You know better than that!" David shouted back "Where there's one ya see there's two ya don't! But all I SEEN was these five!"

"Were not gonna stand em off HERE! Make every shot count!" Tom bellowed over the din, as if the rest of us hadn't thought of that already! David yelled he was going to circle around and try to cut off the approaching warriors and suddenly took off for the left of our position and disappeared into the trees before I could tell him to hold his ground.

I was sure he was only trying to find safer cover for himself and leave us to do the fighting. He may have been an Indian fighter back in Ohio but these were Blackfoot warriors! And this was their territory!! One nod to Long Walker and he understood I wanted him to keep an eye on David. And it was a good thing he did, because it was what saved us from being caught by surprise from the rear.

Saul and Cole had taken shelter behind the boulder with Tom and as always were working as a team. Saul was the better shot so he would shoot, and Cole was faster at loading and would load for him. Between them they kept up a pretty impressive rate of fire!

Sam had finally noticed he had an arrow in his arm and reached up and snapped it off as though it was a slight annoyance and threw it in the direction of the charging Indians yelling "Here!! Try that one again!!" and took up two of his pistols just as a warrior leapt out from behind a tree not a hundred feet away. Sam let him have both pistol charges, reducing the warrior to a groaning heap on the forest floor.

I couldn't see what the others were doing after the start of the fight, there was too much confusion and smoke and noise! Long Walker, who never understood this white way of fighting, had found the enemy to our rear, sneaking up on us and charged several warriors alone!

As he ran from tree trunk to tree trunk, he shot arrows from his short bow, leaving his musket instead of reloading it. As he ran by one of the Blackfoot he had just shot he effortlessly recovered his arrow from the mans chest and reloaded for the next warrior in his path, putting the arrow through his throat. When he tried to recover his arrow another warrior jumped on him from behind. I shot him just as he tackled Long to the ground.

When the smoke cleared I saw Long take his war club and bash in the warrior's skull before moving on. By the time I had reloaded Long had done for another enemy in the same fashion, and was now running back our way to help with the group that had now flanked our position, pinning us down.

As He ran towards us Long took his tomahawk from his belt and while running full speed let it fly and buried it in the back of one warrior I did NOT see who was nearly on top of us. I heard shots to the rear and left of our position and assumed it was David encountering more attackers there.

Then all was quiet. The only sounds being the heaving breath of my crew and the sound of men reloading weapons.

I saw a feather sticking out of a bush a few yards away, and saw it creep slightly to the left, so I slowed my breathing and focused the sight on Long Stick about a foot below where the feather slightly crept along in the brush. I let out my breath slowly as I squeezed the trigger and felt the rifle buck in my hands. I heard a yelp from the brush and the feather disappeared from sight.

I looked to my right and Sam was on his back with a warrior on top of him with a knife in one hand and a tomahawk in the other poised to strike.

"Tom! He's all yours!" I shouted but Tom already had it handled and a split second after I yelled I heard his Hawken .54 caliber *BOOM* behind me. The warrior slumped over on top of Sam, who wriggled out from under him and slit the man's throat with the dirk he carried.

Then the chaos started all over again. As I was reloading and Sam gathered his weapons, I heard a shot go off right behind me and felt the weight of a man hit me full force in the back.

I dropped my rifle and while I rolled out from under the man I saw the big hole in the side of his head oozing blood. I looked and Cole was the one who had shot the warrior as he leapt onto my back to kill me. Cole was a dead shot with those pistols of his! Saul fired a shot behind him, at some target none of the rest of us could see and must have hit it cause he turned and started to reload!

By now the scene was complete chaos and smoke! Cole stood up and leapt over the log to meet another attacker who had crept up while we were busy with reloading. He took a slash at the warrior with his knife but the Indian ducked under it, rolled, and sunk his knife into Cole's thigh before coming back to his feet.

He whirled to jump on top of Cole but Cole was ready and flipped his bowie through the air and deep into the warriors chest, dropping him instantly. Cole stood for a moment ROARING in pain and rage as he took the warrior's knife from his leg, and buried it deep in the dead man's back!

Saul dropped his rifle against the rock and ran to his partner, who was having a hard time walking let alone running back to cover. He picked Cole up and more flung him than carried him back behind the boulder they had used for cover.

As Saul was about to make the cover of the rock himself, two arrows appeared in his back and he fell just short of cover. Cole reached out and took him by the arm and dragged him the rest of the way. By then I had Long Stick loaded again, but the bowman had disappeared in the smoke.

Then there was only silence.

My ears ringing from the constant gunfire and shouts of the men, I looked around and saw no more attacking enemies. Long Walker stood from the brush about a hundred feet away and whooped his victory over the Blackfoot warriors. I heard the moaning of the dying and injured men around me, and a few seconds later hoof beats retreating to the east of our position.

I stood and located the retreating warrior and raised Long Stick to fire and felt a deep stab of pain go through my side.

I ignored it as I let out my breath and took aim at the rapidly shrinking target and let the ball fly! A moment later the warrior toppled off his horse and fell in a slump on the ground and didn't move. The warrior's horse, feeling the weight off his back, slowed to a trot and then stopped altogether a few hundred yards away out in the open grassland.

"There's one redskin that won't be tellin' no tales!" I heard David yell as he came up from behind me. He had a chicken egg sized lump and a deep gash in his forehead and a nasty looking cut across his ribs, and was limping significantly on one leg.

"Where'd *you* run off to??" I shouted rather gruffly

"Back yonder where they was tryin' to outflank us" He explained as he pointed to the two dead warriors "Them two there got past me before I run up on the others!"

"How many were there?" I asked. "Here see fer yerself man!" David grinned and tossed three ears at my feet. I just nodded, satisfied he had not just scooted off to save himself.

Long Walker was singing and doing a dance of victory I had seen before as he went around to those he had killed taking their scalps.

Samuel leaned over one warrior and found him still breathing, if you could call choking on a pink bubbling froth breathing. "Too far gone to waste lead on ye," he growled as he shoved his knife between two ribs into the man's heart to end him.

Sam had recently taken up the habit of scalping his kills like the Indians did, and by the looks of the job he did on this one, he was getting good at it.

Cole and Saul had been doing it for years, as there was a bounty paid at rendezvous for Indian scalps. Cole hobbled over to the one who had tried backstabbing him, and took a handful of the warriors hair in one hand and made a circle cut around the man's skull, and with a quick jerk had the warriors hair free.

Tom was in the process of trying to remove the arrows from Saul's shoulder blade when he looked at me. "Silas mind your side, yer bleedin' man!" Sure enough when I looked down I had blood all down my side. I lifted my shirt to find a nasty gash just below my ribs, though it wasn't too deep it only added to the pain I still felt from the ribs I had broken in my fall.

It seemed that Tom and Long Walker were the only ones who WERE NOT injured in the fight. And it was a good thing Tom WASN'T hurt as he had at one time gone to medical school for the Army and had better knowledge of patching up wounds than any of us.

Chapter 4

Later that evening around the fire, Tom finished up doctoring on the crew while Long and I cooked some meat over it. Some venison we had jerked a while back Long put in a pot to boil with just enough of the flour that was left to make a thin soup.

Long had gathered up what of our horses he could find, as well as a few of the Indian ponies. "We lost two pack horses, one with traps one with food." Long informed me.

"Were gonna have to track them horses come first light" Tom pointed out "Or were purt' near sunk for the season! And I doubt any of you are up to the job."

"Were about sunk NOW" Saul blurted. His shoulder was bandaged and bloody but Tom had said he was lucky both arrows hit his shoulder blade and didn't penetrate far.

Cole had taken a belt off one of the dead warriors to make a tourniquet for his leg, but it was still bleeding badly. "Were damn shore down for a few days fer healin" He strained through the pain "That iron hot enough yet Tom?" "I suppose it is." Tom replied. "Well git on with it man, I'm leakin' bad here!" Cole laid on his belly "HOLD ME DOWN BOYS!" He shouted and bit down on the leather strap of his rifle sling.

Tom knelt one knee on Cole's back while Long Walker and I held his arms, and Sam sat on his feet. Tom held his breath as he put the hot knife to Cole's wound to sear it.

Cole made no sound and only struggled a little against the pain until the job was done. Then when we released him he beat his fists against the ground and cussed every "back stabbin liver eatin' lice infested heathen" in the mountains at the top of his lungs!

Samuel had insisted on keeping the arrowhead Tom took from his shoulder wound as a trophy. "Coulda kilt me," He said "But it dint! Where I come from that's considered good luck!" How he could makes jokes while in such pain we never could understand. Must be the Scot in him.

"Sure and I could use some whiskey about now" David commented through gritted teeth, "Me noggins beatin' twice as fast as me heart! I ougtta go back n kill that one again for hittin' me with that stone ax!"

"Be glad it WAS a stone ax and you got a hard head, me boy!" Sam told him "If it had been steel you'd be dead as yer brudder!"

"Dontcha be talkin' about me brudder!" David spat "But I suppose yer right about that, Id still drink the whiskey if'n I had it though!"

All in all Long Walker counted up eleven dead Blackfoot warriors. With that number of enemies it was surprising we had no more casualties and none killed in our party. But like I said these boys knew how to fight!

There wasn't much more conversation around the fire that evening. Supper was thin and morale was low even though we had been victorious in the day. David had gone off by himself as was his habit. Long had resumed his search for the pack horses. "Good moon to track." he said as he walked out of camp. It was a full moon so I didn't argue. It wouldn't have done much good anyway as once Long made up his mind to do something there was no more discussion he just went off and did it!

"Its gonna be a week or so before any of you are gonna fully be up to working again" Tom told me while we smoked by the fire that evening. "Saul and Cole are down for maybe two."

"The rest of us are gonna have to make up the difference." I said slowly. "We can still make a good go of it if we keep running the traps while we recover from this. We're just lucky this bunch didn't have guns. We got lucky."

"I fully agree with ya there. Well! By my tally" Tom interjected "were a good bit ahead of this time last season, Its not long before the winter is done and we'll be at rendezvous. Maybe we should rest up a bit more."

"You may be right," I admitted.

A couple hours later Long returned with *both* of our pack horses and a few more Indian ponies as well! That would come in handy for trade at the rendezvous!

Evidently this had been a hunting party that David had come across while working his traps, because one of the Indian mustangs had a leg of an elk tied to its saddle. I thought to myself *That's why they didn't have guns. It is lucky this was not a war party or David would be dead, maybe all of us.* But all I said was "At least we will eat well while we recover."

"We better find some better place to do it." Tom commented wisely "These boys may have friends nearby that come lookin!" And he was right.

Once we had taken a day to recover a bit and lick our wounds, we moved the camp to a defensible place with our backs to a steep canyon on a good flowing stream. We had a good point to overlook the valley below and felt confident no one could sneak up on us without our knowing it.

One morning I awoke early from the dreams that were coming more often now. The woman who needed me to save her. From what I could never remember.

Each time I felt the vividness of it and wished that I could remember more. But as dreams do they would fade into obscurity once I had been awake for but a short time. Each time though I felt a lingering urgency and anxiety that I must find this woman, and what it was she needed rescue from.

One particular morning I sat apart from the others, as was my habit, with hardtack and beans contemplating this, when Tom decided to join me. "You give up on coffee now?" He asked "I done called ya four times already and ya dint even seem to hear!"

I took the tin cup of the strong black liquid and thanked him. "You got somethin' on your mind I can tell." he added. I took a sip of the coffee, it was good this morning even though we had no sugar. "Yeah Tom I do..."

Chapter 5

With the coming of spring, there was a burst of activity in the village of the Crow. Black Coyote was eager to go on the hunt; not only for game but for any trespassers on Crow land, white or otherwise. The Cheyenne had been encroaching further into Crow lands as they fought over hunting grounds to the south with the Comanche and Kiowa.

With the death of White Eyes a new Elder had been elected Chief. Stone Bear was now the leader of this band of the Crow. He had been a friend of White Eyes before his death and thought much the same. He also agreed more needed to be known about the whites men who were appearing more and more in Apsaalooke lands. The Blackfeet and their cousins the Piegan to the north, the Ute in the valleys over the tall mountains, all reported having noticed an increase in the number of whites in their lands.

White Medicine Bear had counseled the Elders that white men in their lands would be a good thing for the people. "The whites bring iron tools and trade beads, and blankets of wool as warm as a buffalo robe, it is true. But they also will bring guns. Guns will bring prosperity to the Apsaalooke people. The guns will bring security from the other tribes. The guns will bring much game to the fires." He had explained.

Stone Bear asked one day, "How can we trust these words? The whites come and take without asking. They hunt our game and take our furs. They seem to want to take, not to trade!"

"Some are greedy and only come to take from these lands it is true," White Medicine Bear replied "They come only to take the beaver to trade with other whites across the big water to the east. Others only wish to trade, and live in peace with the Apsaalooke. Is there not room to live in peace?"

Black Coyote could hold his tongue no longer *"In PEACE??"* He stood and raised his voice so all could hear. "I have had a vision of the

25

peace that whites will bring the People! They will come in numbers as many as the flies on a dead carcass! They will come and cover the land like the snows in winter! First one flake falls and is unnoticed, then more fall, and then the land is covered! They fall like the deep winter when one cannot see the ears of his horse in front of him! If the People try to make trade with the whites and have a peace.. there will be no more room for the People!! This was my vision!"

When he finished speaking many people began to shout. Some wanted to make war on the whites, while others wanted to make trade with them, and try to secure a peace that would give the Apsaalooke the right to dictate where the whites could go and not go. Others suggested making a peace that would limit and tax the whites for the furs they took. Others suggested making a pact with the Cheyenne and the Blackfeet, Ute and other tribes to drive the whites back across the great river!

Finally Stone Bear held his hand up and waited for all to quiet themselves before he spoke. "The Council must talk of these things as White Eyes wished., and I will speak to Angry Face Woman and Broken Bow. They may be able to me more of how these whites live."

Some began shouting again but Stone Bear only raised his voice louder over them. "Black Coyote and Chasing Horse will go and scout the summer hunting ground, where he chased the white before winter." Soon it became more and more quiet as he continued. "He will go to make sure the high valley is still safe for the people to hunt and fish as we always have!"

He then turned to Black Coyote. "You must make sure there are no tracks of the whites, or the Comanche or Kiowa. And you will take White Medicine Bear with you in case you find any that are there. He will speak his words of peace." Black Coyote only nodded his acceptance of this edict, though his face showed anger.

Stone Bear went on "Two Crows and Grassy Hair will go back again to the Adobe Lodges in the low land and bring back news of what happens there now that the winter has passed. If others choose to go as well they are free to go."

Two Crows looked at Grassy Hair and nodded, he knew who else he would ask to go on this scout with them. "Buffalo Rider will go to Angry Face Woman and Broken Bow and tell them to come tomorrow at first light so that I may speak with them." Buffalo Rider immediately got up and left at this point while Stone Bear went on. "What does White Medicine Bear say of this?"

"It is wise of Stone Bear to act with caution," White Medicine Bear replied "This will show the whites that the Crow are strong *and* wise, and will give the Crow a strong arm with which to govern their lands as they choose!"

These words pleased Stone Bear, but would only appease many of the others for the time being. Stone Bear waved at Paints Her Face and she brought him his pipe. "That is all I have to say." he said, and took a stick from the fire to light his pipe.

Chapter 6

It now has been several weeks since our fight with the Blackfoot, and the warmer weather has brought a change in activity to me and my men. In that time, the men wounded had healed significantly, and were able to resume their trapping duties, with one exception.

Saul's shoulder wound was worse than we had originally thought. Apparently a small piece of the obsidian arrow head had stayed embedded in his shoulder blade. It had become infected for a while leaving Saul in camp to heal from fever for a while. While he fought the fever he complained of pains in his back whenever he lifted his arm. "Feels like its grating on bone" He had said.

I had to assign him to only light duties around camp now. He would skin and stretch the hides we brought in and took on a major portion of the cooking. Until he could have a doctor remove the chip of obsidian from his back, he could no longer trap or hunt, and in reality would be seriously hampered in a fight.

With the weather turning warmer due to the coming of spring we gathered all the traps and were concentrated on the bundling and baling of the furs for the trip to the rendezvous near the low pass in Wyoming territory. Once again the talk of the men turned to what they would do with their shares.

One afternoon I noticed Tom carefully cleaning the skull of a fox by the fire. I sat and poured myself some coffee and watched him for a moment before my curiosity got the better of me. "What ya gonna do with all them skulls Tom?" I asked "I always wondered about that."

All he said was "Oh I got plans for em... call it my retirement plan."

"Fine you keep your secrets... God knows I sure got mine." I took a sip of the hot coffee and it was bitter today. "Any sugar left?" I asked "Nope, Long used the last of it this morning." Tom replied.

"Speaking of him where is he today? You seen him?" I asked.

Tom shook his head "Nope I aint seen him since yesterday come to think on it."

"Yeah, knowing him though, he probably found some new trail or footprint he couldn't explain." I mused. "Hes always off on some business known only to him." Which was true.

Long Walker had that name for a reason, he didn't like staying in one place too long. Plus he was a scout, so I assumed he was off scouting. "Well let me know when he comes in, would ya? I got something I wanna talk to him about."

I looked around camp to be sure no one was within earshot before I went on. "When we get to the rendezvous this year I need to find someone who can look over this map and tell me what the words are. I know Long can speak Spanish but I don't think he can read it.. I want him to scout some honest Mexican to tell us what the map says. The details and markings might be something very important."

"The Green river is a bit far north to be finding Mexicans, let alone one I'd trust to read on a map we don't want no one to know about," Tom pointed out. "Might have more luck down south a ways."

I nodded and thought for a moment, sipping my coffee as it quickly got cold, "You might be right. Long Walker don't like the rendezvous anyway. Maybe I should have him go south and find us someone down that way. I mean, it is his peoples territory."

"You need a few more men if what I hear about them Indians down that a way is true." Tom was always the one to point out the negative side of things. He was a good balance to my more impulsive side. "Them Kiowa and Comanche are bloodthirsty when it comes to their territory. Besides there's a lotta mountains between here and there. Were gonna need better horses too!"

"I disagree Tom, I think were going to need to be pretty stealthy and a smaller party of men is probably best to do that with. I think we will be okay as long as we are careful," I told him "I'm gonna get some of them Appaloosas from Dick Cooper, and they're gonna cost quite a bit. But from what I hear they are the best mountain horse a man can have. So if were gonna be goin' through that many mountains I want all of you to have the best horse we can get under ya. *Thats* gonna cost some coin! Better to stick with the best of what we have now, and not bring in too many more."

Just then I saw some birds take off out of the brush like it was on fire and I took up Long Stick and cocked the hammer, while Tom pulled out his pistol. Hearing a familiar bird call, I relaxed and let the hammer down easy. "It's Long.." I told Tom. "I told him no more sneakin' up on me. I told him call like a whipporwill so's I could tell he was coming." I told him. "*Since he cant just yell HELLO THE CAMP like everyone else!*" I shouted to Long.

Long stepped out from behind a tall pine and walked silently into camp. "You say make the sound of whipporwill, so I do, now that not good enough?" He asked with a hint of a smile in his dark eyes.

"Ya know Long ifn I didn't know better I'd say you just made a joke! Now that can't be!" Tom said.

"What means 'joke'?" Long asked as he reached for the coffee pot.

"Uh huh, riiiight." Tom chuckled "So where ya been man? Come on spit it out! Don't make us wait, ya been gone since yesterday!"

"I find tracks of war party going south. Crow. Maybe go to fight Cheyenne or Comanche."

"If they was goin' away from us why didn't ya just come back?" Tom asked

"Five warriors took different path, to here I think. But they go by and meet with another party different than before. And go on south from there, I think to meet first party I tracked." Long explained.

"When are the others supposed to be back Tom?" I asked. "Anytime now I'd say." Tom just nodded and picked up a turkey he had killed earlier that day, to pluck and put on the spit.

"Yep they left before first light this morning to go for the last of the furs, they should be back anytime 'tween now and dark probly." Tom confirmed.

A little ways off in the distance, we heard the distinctive sound of a horses hoof glancing off a rock in the trail, and soon Samuel rode in on his little mustang mare, leading two others loaded with bales of furs. "Got back quick as I could!" Samuel shouted as he rode up to the camp. "I seen a war party headed this way, looked like Crow, maybe thirty of em!" He said as he dismounted and began to unload the bales from the pack horses. "And they was painted up lookin' like they mean business!"

"Id say its past time to go." I told Tom as I got up to help Sam unload the bales.

The others began to drift in about an hour after Sam, but none of them reported any sign of Indians on their trail that day.

"We'll have to wait a day or two before we can leave," I told them. "I told Paul to meet us here with his men and he should be on his way here now."

Saul took the turkey and put it on the spit to roast. "Should be done enough in about an hour id say. You makin' biscuits Tom? I think if we all put in what we got left we can have some made for morning and save some time."

"Of course I'm makin' the biscuits! None of you jack fools can make a decent biscuit if it'd save yer life!"

While the rest of the men sat and socialized by the fire, I asked Long about the others. "Any more of Paul's men coming with him ya think Long? We could use the help, plus the safety of numbers with all these furs going through Crow lands."

"The rest work more north, Paul tells me. Going to go direct to rendezvous from there. Save time." Long responded. "One man, Cherokee Thunder Hand, was killed last month. Scalped by the Crow while hunting."

David stood up suddenly and sarcastically asked "I wonder who is gonna get *his* share when all is said and done!!" and turned towards his tent.

I turned to face him, I done had enough! "I'm gonna ignore that McNeil, but I'm getting mighty tired of your sullen attitude! Once you are paid for you and your brothers share at rendezvous I'm done with you, and you are done with me! You got that??"

"Why *YES Your Majesty!*" David spat over his shoulder, "Just remember it was me who lost his brudder, not you!"

"That's enough David you need to stay out of the whiskey, you're drunk!" Samuel put himself between David and me "Go now! And shut yer mouth or I'll shut it for ya!"

David walked off sullenly towards his tent but couldn't resist another jab "This business ain't done till its done Silas Horn! We will finish it at rendezvous!"

Once he was out of earshot Tom said quietly "Your gonna have to watch yer back Silas! That one has the look of a backstabber ifn I ever seen one!"

"I tend to agree with ya there" I nodded "But right now we may need his rifle yet. There's a lot of Indian country 'tween here and the Green."

Just then Cole rode in with a couple pack horses in tow loaded with bales of furs and the business at hand turned to helping him unload and organize his bales with the others.

The sun clung to the peaks it seemed as the last rays of the glowing orange light illuminated the valley with an array of yellows and golds in beams of light that shone through the clouds. The rest of the evening was filled with the making of plans for the days long trip to the Green River for the rendezvous. Once we had all eaten dinner and had a pass of the whiskey jug, we talked plans for the next couple days.

The next morning, breakfast was coffee and cold meat and hardtack. David took his and went off alone again as was his habit now.

The rest of the men seemed optimistic in the face of the trip we were going to undertake through hostile territory.

Now, in a camp full of men such as we were, one of the last things to be packed up is the coffee pot. And just as Saul was about to pour the last cup, we heard a shout from down the trail we were camped near. "Don't pack up that pot yet old man you got thirsty men a comin' in!"

Saul, never one to miss the beat shouted right back "Old man hell! Come in and we'll make another pot!" And soon Paul McVeigh and a three others rode into camp trailing pack horses laden with heavy packs. "We got cold meat and biscuits too if'n yer hungry!" Saul added.

"Not Tom's biscuits I hope!" One of the others shouted. It was Adam Forsythe. "Last time I had one o *Tom's* biscuits I broke a tooth!" Adam was a Canadian of English birth. He had, until a couple years earlier, been in the employ of The Hudson's Bay Company in the east, and had found his way to the Rockies with a group of french Canadians that were pushing in from the east. With him, rode Andre LaFleur and Pierre Montrose, also former Company men.

Adam was a wiry little man about four inches over five feet tall. He was skinny as a fence rail, with a sort of pinched up look to his face, which he kept clean shaven even in the rough country. Although English by birth, he had spent quite a few years as a younger lad, with a group of Seneca near the Great Lake Huron in the eastern regions. Not only had he adopted their manner of dress, but also the practice of plucking all but the top patch of hair from his head, which he kept in a long braid down his back. This was not only a cultural practice among some eastern tribes, but was also seen as a taunt to ones enemies, tempting them to come and try to take it!

He wore leggings of deerskin, with a blue woolen breech cloth intricately beaded with the patterns of the eastern woodlands tribes. Over his tea cloth shirt he wore a trade blanket capote. In addition to his .54 caliber Hawken rifle, he carried a pistol, tomahawk, and an Algonquin war club he had taken as a prize in a battle with the Mohawk.

"Was a time you *had teeth* Adam? I don't remember ever seein' ivory in your face!" Tom shot back.

"Broke the last one on one o your biscuits Tom!" Adam dismounted and tied his buckskin to a sapling near the other horses. "Its good to see ya still breathin' Tom!" He added and put out his hand for a shake.

"Good to see you above ground still too Adam! I see ya still got yer topknot there!" And shook Adam's hand with a vigor.

Adam replied with a smile, "Yep I sure do! I think once them Indians get up close to me and see I'm a white man they don't know what to think!! Many a time I shot one while he just stood there with his mouth open like he seen a ghost! I am what ya might call an eeenigma!"

Andre broke in at this point and said "Dont give yourself too much credit Adam! Been a time or two I've had to keep em off your back too! While you was pickin' trinkets off the dead ones!"

"Shut up frenchie!" Adam laughed and nodded at me, "Tom, Silas, I'd like you to meet Andre LaFleur. Quite possibly the most annoying Frenchman you will ever meet!"

"And here I thought ya didn't like me!" Andre grinned as he put out his hand to Tom.

Tom found himself shaking hands with a squat, broad man, shorter than most, and wider as well, dressed in fringed buckskins, a woolen pea-coat, and a pointed woolen cap. Poking out from under his hat were locks of sandy brown hair which matched the beard that hung halfway down his chest. Though he was portly in appearance the grip of his handshake belied a power hidden amid his mass.

"Good to meet you." Tom said curtly. He normally didn't like Frenchmen, as they were the enemy during the war. *We'll just see if this ones any better.* He thought.

"And this is Silas Horn," Adam pointed to me. "Hes the head boss here." I shook Andre's hand and nodded at Adam. "I see Montrose is still as silent as ever! Not sure how to take that!"

Michael Montrose, or 'Monty' to most, just nodded and lifted a hand in greeting. He was just walking up to the fire after tying his horses near the others.

Monty also dressed in buckskins, but wore a coat of sheepskin that he had made for himself, from the skins of the big horn sheep that were numerous in these mountains. Being taller by a head than most men Monty had an intimidating presence in most company.

His hair, blonde in color, was wild and unkempt, sticking out from his head at odd angles, knotted from the wind and elements. He also carried a Hawken style rifle, but his was a .58 caliber, and he carried two pistols in his belt. He wore no hat, preferred to stand when most sat, and never uttered a word. At least none that any here had ever heard.

"Coffee will be half cooked in a few minutes. Come set a spell and tell us. How'd you boys do? Y'all gonna make us rich again this year?" Tom asked

Paul tossed a piece of hardtack to his men and shoved half of one in his mouth before he spoke with his mouth full. "We done good by most standards I'd say" Pausing to chew a couple times, "Got these nine here loaded down and six more with the others. Standing Bear brought in three lions and a couple big grizzlies. All in all not a bad take!"

"He still goin' after em in their den while they're sleepin'?" I asked "Tom this is the craziest thing listen to this!"

"Sure enough!" Paul confirmed "I can't tell if hes crazy or smart, but he sure does! Goes right in after em and sometimes it takes a while to dig em or pull em out, but that crazy Indian knows what hes doing!"

"Just sounds insane to me!" Tom exclaimed. "Have much trouble with the Crow?" he asked. "Think we'll have much trouble on the trail?"

"Not much," Paul answered "we seen a couple hunting parties, but thanks to your tent camouflage technique, they never saw us, and one party was only a couple hundred feet off at the time! I wasn't so sure about that to start with but damn sure worked like you said!"

"That coffee 'bout done?" Adam pointed at the bubbling pot. "Its gonna boil over in a minute!"

Saul took the pot off the fire and drizzled a little cold water into the top to help settle the grounds. "Help yourself! Hope ya like it thick enough to chew!"

Paul poured himself a cup, passed the pot to Adam, and continued his report, "Two Knives is gonna meet us at rendezvous with the rest of the men. They gonna have it on the Green where Horse Creek flows into it this year, better grazing they say. Hes gonna scout out a good spot a bit off from the main camp for us."

Adam spoke up at this point. "We got a couple new fellas with us too. Company men that got separated from their party up north a ways. We found em half starved and runnin' from Blackfeet at the time. Ones a black fella, but he weren't no slave and he knows trappin', that's a fact!"

I lit my pipe while I listened, "Good!" I said between puffs "We can use a few more good men! We are going to be short handed after rendezvous I think."

David shot me a dirty look but didn't say anything for once.

Once the newcomers had their fill of coffee and breakfast, the men resumed their packing up to leave for rendezvous. The sun rose higher, a bright amber icon rising over the broken teeth of the mountain range. The mists gave themselves over to the warmth of day and hid themselves from the sun in the shadowed valleys.

Horses stamped at the picket line, swishing their tails at the hoards of biting flies. Birds flew about the warming skies, rejoicing in song at the coming of spring. All about was the smell of new life. Buds were starting to bloom on the trees, flowers beginning to show hints of their painted faces. And the men, filled with the new hope that comes from surviving the winter in such a wild inhospitable place, were laughing and joking, reveling in the warm sunny temperatures, and the promise of new fortunes to come. In that moment, we were kings!

When all was done, the meat gone and coffee pot empty, the fire was put out and everyone mounted up for the long ride to the Green. We rode mostly in silence, all leading pack horses loaded with our fortunes. Long Walker, as always, ran ahead and scouted for any sign of trouble along the trail.

I could only think of the days to come. What would the map reveal once it was translated?

I had started to form an idea in my mind, but I had no proof, so I kept that idea even from Tom.

The one thing that was for sure, was that we had a lot of work to do in a very short time before the winter came again to prevent us.

Chapter 7

The skies were angry and dark as we came to the Green and Horse Creek camp for rendezvous. Rain came down in torrents at times, then after, the winds would come and chill us to the bone. We found a likely campsite in a stand of aspen on a little hill overlooking the sprawling temporary city that had sprung up out of the grasses on the banks of the Green River.

Scattered across both banks of The Green and Horse Creek were encampments of Indian tribes in their tipis. Tribes friendly to the English and French from the north as well as those from down in the Columbia river valley all came to trade.

Across the river was laid out a military looking camp of wall tents and pavilion tents of The American Fur Company, Hudson's Bay Company, and Canadian Fur companies as well as numerous other traders. It was not hard to spot traders row this year, even through the rain and mists and smoke of the campfires.

Rendezvous this year seemed to be starting on quite a muddy and miserable note with the early and frequent rains of the spring. This was the Rockies after all and it was said that if you don't like the weather here to wait five minutes or travel five miles. I doubted that day that either would help.

We stopped for a moment while I pointed out to Tom "Here take these horses and get the men settin' up camp over in them aspens over there... they can start dryin' out by the fire while I go down and have a look see." I told him

"What? You're goin' now?" he asked as he took the lead to my pack horses, "Whatever and whoever will be there tomorrow after all this rain dries up."

"Yeah, I wanna go see who's in charge of this mess this year, see if I can find an old friend." I told him while I reigned my horse around towards the big camp. The little mustang really didn't like me at that moment as I'm sure he too wanted to stop and get out of the wind. "Just a little more, boy" I told him as he started to trod on.

It didn't take me long to find my way to traders row.

Now, traders row is what we called the line of tents put up by the Companies and Traders that camp to buy the furs and resupply the men at the end of each season. Even in bad weather such as today one could find anything from flour to firearms, and whiskey to women. Though these rendezvous were mostly comprised of men for the first few years, a few had started to recruit women to come out as 'camp followers' did with the armies for centuries.

Today I was only interested in one particular tent. And it didn't take me long to find the hand carved wooden sign I was looking for. *"Clayton Stroebel, Agent, American Fur Company"*

When I found it I dismounted and called quietly, "Clay! Ho Clayton! You at home here?"

A deep voice called back "Come in if yer friendly Im too busy stayin' dry to go out! Tie up yer horse around the back!" As I was tying my horse to the picket line I found there Clay shouted again.

"Who is that? Who is dumb enough to come a callin' in the middle of Noah's flood?" He poked his head out through the tent flap and immediately smiled. "Silas P. Horn! I shoulda knowed it was you!"

"Oh so now I'm dumb huh? That what yer sayin?" I shot back. Clay just smiled bigger and opened the tent flap wide for me, "I don't have to! You just said it!" He laughed then added "Well come on then, get in here out the rain ya old grizzly!"

When I stepped into the tent a wave of heat slapped me in the face. The inside of the tent was divided into two parts. This was the rear of the tent where off to one side was a pallet bed covered with buffalo robes and the other side was a small iron stove. "I ain't seen a wood stove in near 2 years!" I told him.

"Yeah, I got a bigger wagon this year. I'm getting too old to be in all this cold and wet without a good stove now a days!' He explained, then said louder "Mouse! Come back here!"

He motioned at a small table with two casks for seats "Have a sit down, don't worry it ain't powder in them casks so ya can smoke if ya like"

I just shook my coat off and stood dripping, "I think ill wait till I stop drippin' first!" I said as I sat down.

An Indian woman came in from the store front area, and went to put a pot on the stove and stirred it. "Don't mind her," Clay said "She don't talk.' He went on to explain "Shes Shoshone, but the Kiowa took her in a raid when she was young. I guess she put up such a ruckus they cut out her tongue to keep her quiet."

"Mouse?" I asked

"Well I don't know what her name is, she never could tell me, that's just what I call her. She don't know English too good so she don't know no difference. Mouse, go and get another cup from the front for my friend," he instructed her.

"Stores kinda small this year Clay," I mentioned pointedly, "Not doin' too good with The Company?" To this he just gave a chuckle and replied, "This is just the overflow and high value stuff. The real store is next door, tents twice as big this year. I done TOLD ya I had a bigger wagon!"

"That you did." I nodded. Just then the squaw came back with a tin cup and a jug that could only be whiskey and set them on the little table. Clay took the cork from the jug and poured two cups half full and shoved one at me. "To the beaver!" He said loudly and downed his drink while Mouse went to cooking on the wood stove. I took a sip and set mine back down.

"I didn't come to get drunk Clay," I told him "I gotta get back to the men. Its only information I seek now and then business tomorrow." and took another sip.

Clay poured more into his and shouted "To the King!" and downed another slug of the fire water. Then said under his breath, "May he suffer the gout!" and slammed his cup down on the table. "*Now*, what do you want to know my friend?" Clay was always a boisterous man. He was a medium built man in his prime, though his long brown hair and beard were streaked with gray. He wore buckskin trousers and tall black boots. His shirt of calico was tied at the waist with a beaded belt of some Indian design similar to the wampum belts I had seen back in the east. Years of outdoors living had worn lines in his face that made him appear much older than his thirty nine years.

Most who met him said it was his eyes that they remembered most. Piercing blue. Like the walls of an ice cave, and always taking in everything about his surroundings even when he drank. "Whores are downhill on the row this year if that's..."

"Not after whores Clay!" I cut him off, maybe a little too gruffly but I was very tired and grumpy with the bad weather. "Who is number one this year? Who's is charge of this mess?" I asked.

"The Company has put Ol Two Toes Brown in charge! Can't ya tell? Everybody's all camped willy nilly anywhere like!" Clay took another slug of whiskey and continued "No organization, just pick as you please!"

I nodded and broke in again. "Yeah it looked like it when we rode in. You hear tell of Spotted Pony or Big Dog. Or maybe Dick Cooper yet?"

"Not yet, I ain't. But if I know Spotted Pony at all he'll be here here soon, Dick too, with them big Nez Perce horses of his! They getting pretty popular round these parts!" He poured another drink for us both and Mouse came and set two bowls of the stew she had been making down on the table.

"That's what I was wantin to talk to ya about Clay." I said and took another swig of the whiskey. "I want some of them appaloosas myself. I was hopin' Dick would be here with a bunch again this year so Im glad to hear you say that." Clay had turned his attention to the stew but nodded grunted that he was listening. "I got plans to go down south into some new mountains this year and Im gonna need some good horseflesh under me and my men. I may need someone to help me finance that."

Clay swallowed and wiped his beard with his hand before he spoke. "You know I'll do the best I can fer ya, Silas, but speakin' of finances, how'd you and yer boys do this year?"

"Id say we done pretty good! Got fourteen pack-horses loaded with just furs. Granted some are a mix of coyotes, cats and a couple bears, but most of em are just beaver. I would'a had more but I had to hide some cause of Indians."

Clay nodded scratching his beard. "Would be better if ya had them others, price of beaver has gone down again this year. You have much Indian trouble this year?" He asked.

For the next couple hours I told him the story of my adventure over and through the mountain; my capture and escape from the Crow, and the strange so called priest I had met. We talked for hours into the night over bowls of stew and cups of whiskey.

We talked of old times and new techniques, and adventures of years past. The rain had stopped and the crickets had begun their serenade to the night when I realized I had better get back to my men.

When I stepped out of Clay's tent, it was into a world of glowing lanterns and fires scattering the landscape. Voices of men talking loudly over each other as men do who have spent months alone with only their own company.

A drunken trapper stumbled past me muttering something about stolen horses, so I quickly stepped around back to make sure my horse was not one of them. The little bay was still standing where I had left him, three legged in a bit of a snooze. I tightened up the cinch and climbed into the saddle with a grunt, and pointed him up the hill towards the glow of our little camp.

It only took a few minutes and we arrived at the little camp in the trees, and I stripped the little mustang of the saddle and bridle and tied the lead rope to the picket line with the others.

When I got to the fire, I saw Tom had left the coffee pot near by to stay warm. I had a cup to warm up with and smoked my pipe, making plans for the next day, before turning in.

Chapter 8

The morning greeted the mountains like a damp towel. A thick fog covered the land and gave a chill to the air. Only the most determined birds sang their song that morning and it seemed even the sun was reluctant to show its face. Everywhere was the smell of wet earth and campfires and horses.

During the night Dick Cooper had come to camp with Big Dog and Spotted Pony. They had with them an impressive looking herd of appaloosas from the Powder River country. Dick had got word from Clay Stroebel and his partner Bill 'The Bull' Turnbull, that there was a growing interest in these mountain bred appaloosas for use in the fur trade in the Rockies.

I was glad to see Ol Dick had brought so many, and was anxious to go look em over before they were all spoken for. After a quick cup of coffee and some bacon I procured from Clay the night before, Tom and I rode bareback down to where the herd was corralled.

"HellOoo, Dick ya old horse thief, you alive in there?" Tom hollered. A moment later a balding head of dirty blond hair with a reddish beard under piercing gray eyes and a hawk nose poked out from the tent flap.

"Don't tell me that old rumor is still floating around!" Dick shouted back. "Don't let my wife hear ya say that! She's liable to confirm it!" Tom and I just chuckled and slid off our horses. Dick came out barefoot in buckskin pants and long johns and shook our hands.

"Ya came early!" he said "I was just getting round to coffee and bacon myself. Have a set, Ill get mare to rustle up some eggs to go with it and we can talk. Uhh, and *do* do an old friend a favor and start a fire in that pit there? Mare is kinda particular 'bout strangers in her tent. Makes *me* sleep out by the fire sometimes too!"

Tom sniffed and smiled "I don't know why you put up with that Dick." He said quietly.

Dick stretched his back and began "Because..." And Tom and I having heard it before finished it for him "..She *loves* me." and we all got a good chuckle out of that.

"Go on, Ill get the fire goin" Tom said, and Dick went back inside.

Once the fire was goin, and we all had feasted on real hen eggs and bacon and Mare's sourdough bread, Dick leaned back and patted his belly, and loaded his pipe for a smoke. "So what brings you boys by?" he asked. "Sure not to just catch up old times."

"I want some of those horses Dick" I went straight into the business at hand. Dick lit his pipe with a flaming stick from the fire, and listened while I continued. "I think twenty, if you have that to sell, that is. I hoped to talk to you first and have my pick.

"Well why didn't you say so at first?" Dick winked "We could a saved Mare some cookin' and I'd still have half a dozen eggs than I got now." He slapped his knee "Well! Lets go have a look. Now, we *are* talkin' cash money here right?" He looked from Me to Tom and back.

"Nope, gold."I took out a $20 gold piece and flipped it to him over the fire. Even Tom was surprised, I saw his head turn to look at me out of the corner of my eye, "That do for ya?" And winked.

"That'll do!" Dick nodded and bit the coin to authenticate it. "How you getting paid in gold up here in the mountains Silas? Sure and ya don't carry gold around with ya id think."

"I guess its my secret then." I said with a wink, and Dick just repeated, "That'll do, yeah."

"The catch is, that's the only one I got right now... I have to sell my furs and can pay the rest after. That's a deposit." I knew Dick wouldn't have a problem with that, my word had always been good enough for him.

"Yep you know your word is always good with me Silas," Dick confirmed it. "Well, lets go take a look, and you take your pick." He added.

At the rope corral Spotted Pony sat on a tall paint horse watching the herd of about sixty horses. Spotted Pony knew English, that is to say he understood it, but refused to speak it. With his hands he made hand gestures commonly used for tribes who didn't speak each others language to communicate.

When he finished his gestured greeting Dick translated. "He says 'white man comes to take horses, he comes to speak with two mouths, make sure he pay more'"

"Well brother if that's how you feel" I said directly to Spotted Pony "Then lets talk some serious business! Get down off that nag and say it again!"

Spotted Pony sat for a moment staring it seemed directly into my soul before he made any other signs. After a moment he couldn't contain it any longer and broke out into a grin and signed "Wandering Dog funny, Make good trade, fair, and be friends"

I chuckled and shook my head, "I've *heard* you talk English Spotted Pony but you play your games." To this Spotted pony went into a tirade of speech in his native Nez Perce that, translated through Big Dog, roughly amounted to jokes about my virility and prowess in battle, or as he put it, the lack thereof.

"You make all the funny talk you want Pony but the fact remains, I AM ALIVE and that says itself!" I responded. Spotted Pony and Big Dog both had to nod their agreement while Dick stood there with his mouth open.

"I wasn't aware you all knew each other Silas," said after a moment, "And how did you all meet then?"

"We had a disagreement once over the ownership of some horses, but that was years ago now and been settled and done already." I explained.

"Well I'm glad of that!" Dick adjusted his suspenders over his shoulders to a more comfortable position, "Well, what ya think man? Which you want?" He said gesturing to the Appaloosas in the pen.

"They look like good strong horses," Tom spoke first, "Good thick front, looks like they can do mountain up or down pretty good. Wide in the rear too."

"I agree.." I said though I barely heard him. Tom and Dick began to talk prices, but that too faded and lost my interest as I watched the herd of horses in the pen.

My father had taught me what to look for in a mountain horse long ago, and I had learned well. The ripple of a horses flank as it moved, or the way it placed its hooves, could tell you much about the horse. These horses were on average a bit thicker than the ponies we had been riding. Taller by at least three hands, and broader across the chest and flanks.

"These will make great for packing as well. . they're much stronger than the. ." Someone was saying but I wasn't paying attention.

These horses carried themselves as lightly as the stable ponies in the east. They held their heads a bit higher than the horses we were used to and seemed to have an inherent intelligence behind their eyes that I was not accustomed to seeing.

There were about sixty good strong horses in the little herd, all different colors from bays to blacks, and even paints, roan and buckskins, but they all had the spotted rear markings that told of their breeding. And among them stood apart a group of about eighteen that seemed to be the core of the herd.

These were the ones I watched, while the other men continued to talk behind me of business. It is like watching a dance, but in a more slow motion form than we humans are used to. If any other horses in the enclosure whether male or female would get too close to this central band, they would be chased off. The horses in the little band seemed to move as one mind was controlling them, while the others in the pen seemed to be outsiders and were not accepted.

One in particular seemed to be directing the others with his own movements. A big black stallion with simple white spot markings on his rear and a wide blaze to match on his face that looked like a bolt of lightning. He was also a bit larger than the rest, and was undoubtedly its leader.

The others around him though not as large, all seemed to be healthy and intelligent specimens, and though I had only planned on negotiating for twelve good saddle horses, I had to interrupt the others and say "Those there with that big black! Those are my pick! And a few more Tom will pick."

I heard Big Dog behind me "Spotted Pony says you at least know good horses."

"Tom you pick out six for you and you can go get a couple of the boys to round em up after I get em paid for, but ill have to make a better deal on the furs now."

"Ill want to trade some of these we got now too if ya want." I had told Dick, and he agreed on a fair price including the half of the mustang ponies we had.

In the end we made a deal on thirty Appaloosas and Dick marked each one with chalk so everyone else would know those were spoken for. The extra horses being partially in trade for some of our smaller mustangs.

When we got back to camp, the rest of the men were about their morning business around camp, and I gave them each a note that was good for ten dollars on traders row, under my name and signature, and let them all go in their own direction. "Ill bet that McNeil is drunk by noon." Tom commented. I could not take that bet, as I was sure of it as well.

Tom and I took our time when the men had gone, to inventory again, while we loaded the pack horses with our bales, so there would be no mistakes during the sale. Once we got them unloaded at Clay's, Tom would take the horses to Dick's for the trade, and report their value to me later, when I had the money for the purchase.

I spent most of the afternoon with Clay, counting again and sorting, haggling and finding Clay to be the fair trader he was in spite of being my friend. All in all I made a pretty good bit this season, and was sure the men would be happy with their shares as well.. well most of them.

Once the sale was done and Clay had counted out my bounty in coin as agreed, we parted ways with a handshake, and I was off to gather my new string of mounts from Dicks corral. Spotted Pony was there arguing with a french trapper about price, and Big Dog and Long Walker were there with Tom, waiting to help take the appaloosas back to our camp.

Once we had them back to camp and secured to the picket line, we sent the agreed number of ponies back with Big Dog. The camp was empty, of course, as the men had all gone down to take part in the festivities of the event. All but Saul, tending the fire, whose injuries' slow healing kept him close to camp.

"How'd we do boss?" he inquired, "We get a good deal like you said? We all rich men now?"

"Rich enough, I'd say," I told him "Two of them appaloosas are yours. And you get to pick first since the others ain't here... just not that big black with the block head on the end. He's mine."

"Leave it to you to pick the blockhead horse, I swear Silas," he said laughing.

"Ill need your help with one other thing though, Ill need you stand my back when I pay the men. Along with Tom and Long here." I told him. "I'm gonna pay David McNeil first, and have him gone when I pay the others."

"You got it, boss! Whatever you need! Hell, for two of those horses, Ill make him disappear for ya!" he replied.

"Ill keep that in mind, I sure will Saul, but for now, just stand by with your rifle while I get him paid and gone, I don't trust him one bit."

"Me neither." he agreed.

Just then Samuel came into camp loudly stating "Well ya wont have ta worry about that tonight! The lad is pure drunk and passed out behind one of the, shall we say, entertainment establishments down in the hog waller."

The hog waller, is what the lowest point of the hill on which the encampment was set up. Usually the muddiest and most foul smelling area on the row. The filth of wash pots and horsepiss, mixed with the rain and wet weather, of course flowed downhill, and in this case right through the place where the gambling and drinking tents were set. Making it reek with the stench of the sins that were engaged in there. And was a good name for the place as well, considering.

"Well, I'll settle up with him tomorrow then." I shook my head as I counted out Samuel's share into a small leather sack. "Here's your due share, and more than we figured this year I'll say as well."

"Ah and in GOLD no less! I dinnae know ya was paying in GOLD laddie!"

"Well if you're complaining.." I smiled and held out my hand.

"NO no laddie not complainin', not a bit!" He smiled and shook his head. "I'll just have to tuck it further in my sack for now!" As he buried the coin deep in his possibles bag, "This is *horses*!"

"Two of them appaloosas are yours as well Sam, go take your pick." He looked at me with surprise, and went to inspect the horses at the picket line.

"And horses to boot, ye say! Well I'll be buggered. Guess I'll be able to buy a couple more with my wages and have me own little herd to raise!"

The rest of the evening was spent cooking on the fire and swapping stories, passing the whiskey jug, and paying off the men as they each came back from the temporary little town on the river.

When Paul came in I took him aside and paid him for all his men and told him each was to be given a horse of their choice from the mounts we held back from the trade with Dick. This seemed to make everyone happy.

Chapter 9

Black Coyote spent the morning going throughout the camp and talking to his best warriors. Many had publicly supported him in his quest to take a war party against the whites that more and more were encroaching on Crow lands.

By nightfall all but two had agreed to 'go hunting' in the next couple of days and meet up at the high mountain camp near their the southern part of their territory. The plan was to inconspicuously mount a tracking party that would follow the whites when they left the great meeting at the Green River.

His scouts had advised him there were other tribes friendly to the Crow in attendance there, and it would not be wise to attack a camp that had so many in numbers of allies as well as enemy tribes. Walking Cloud, his chief supporter and head scout, had identified the camp of the white who had gotten away from Black Coyote before the winter. He felt confident enough he had left his own son there to keep watch and report to them which direction the party took when they left the gathering.

Now as he sat in the high mountain camp where he came to hunt elk, the warriors began to show up in ones and twos. Each man bringing his own supplies, and weapons of war, on their best horses to mount this expedition. It was a great undertaking but each felt secure in their mind it was the right thing to do.

Two days after the agreement to the secret raid, there were now already twenty seven sturdy warriors in camp, and those had brought news of others that were planning to come in the next couple of days.

Black Coyote was please to see how many had kept their word to come on such a secret mission, many might fear reprisals from the Old Ones, or their women, for going off under false pretenses to ultimately be gone for weeks.

Walking Cloud and Stands with Eagles sat at Black Coyotes fire, set of elk ribs roasting over the fire filling their noses and making their bellies rumble in anticipation, while talking of plans of the mission to come.

"Fast Hare is a good scout, he will know where the whites have gone when we get to the other side of the mountains. I saw the man who was our captive myself and made Fast Hare study his camp and his men so he will not mistake them for any others." Walking Cloud was saying, "Bird Hunter has his hawk and can send him for us to follow if they need to follow more closely and cannot meet with us before we can reach them."

Black Coyote nodded and looked to Stands With Eagles, who then began to speak.

"What if they have gathered more men from the gathering and we become outnumbered?" He asked.

"A Crow warrior on his own land can not be outnumbered," Black Coyote spoke slowly as he wished no misunderstanding, "once a battle is made we have our people to call to come and finish the fight. In the end it will only matter that we are in battle with the whites, it will not matter how that battle began."

Walking Cloud spoke up and added "It is for the good of the whole people, these people are our enemies and they cannot get away with pillaging our lands for their own gain! The more this is allowed to continue with no consequence, it will happen more, and more, as it has with our cousins to the east who now have lost their lands to the whites! NO! This must be done, even if the Old Ones have no stomach for it!"

"And what of the Cheyenne? Or the Kiowa? Or Comanche? What of going farther south and into their territory with only a few to fight?" Stands With Eagles asked.

"We do not wear warpaint." Black Coyote answered "And do not paint our horses for battle. That is for when we are going to war with the Cheyenne, or the Kiowa or Ute. No. If the other tribes do not see us in war regalia we can tell them of what we do in their lands. I am certain they also wish to repel the whites and maybe some arrangement can be made."

"Peace with the Kiowa? With the Comanche? It cannot be done!" Walking Cloud interjected "Those ties were cut many many moons ago and the wound is too deep to repair. I do not think that can be done."

"It will be a risk we will have to take.. every tribe knows of the parlay talks, even in hand signs. We will make do as we can." Black Coyote took the ribs from the fire by the green spit it was roasting on and took his knife to cut himself a piece, and passed the rest to Walking Cloud . "For now we must gather our strength in numbers and make our war medicine."

At that moment Lame Hawk walked into camp to squat by the fire. "I have brought my brothers and my cousin Crow Dog, seven in all, and are camped at the bend of the river with the crossing. We have seen no sign of anyone following after us. I think that Stone Bear has been told of our plans. Night Hawk has decided to not come, and I think he has told Morning Bear of our plans."

Black Coyote stood quickly, "If Morning Bear is told she will surely tell her brother. But what we must think of is what will Stone Bear DO with the information?" He paced a little by the fire as he spoke a bit more to himself than to the others. "He does not have the support in the council to declare us as renegade, and he knows my intention is honorable, Stone Bear will not send warriors after us. If he does they will come only to try to reason with us to abandon this hunt. Perhaps instead we can convince them of our mission and they will join us too. Stone Bears thinking is of that of one who is at the end of his life and is happy that it is so! Many of our men are just beginning and wish to live as we always have. I think many will join us in this mission."

When he had finished speaking, he abruptly walked away from the little group, even forgetting his elk rib meal, and walked to his horse and mounted. For now he would help watch the horses. He had been in charge of the pony herds when he was a boy and he found that being with the horses he could think clearer.

He could not admit it even to himself that he had doubts about this whole plan. He was driven to punish this white man for killing his friends, but had a duty to the Crow people as well, and somehow he must align the two. As he approached Broken Nose he lifted his lance to signal him he would take over his position so the warrior could go and eat, and warm himself by the fire.

It was drawing into evening, and the sun, dropping behind the mountains to the west, shone bright orange in the sky while overhead black clouds threatened to rain down on them. It was then he realized he had forgotten his elk ribs. It would not be the first night he had gone hungry. In truth he believed this cleared his mind and gave him his visions of his path before him. Perhaps tonight he would have a vision, among the storm, and his way would be clear.

Chapter 10

The next morning awoke with all the glory and majesty that can be beheld in the mountains. The sun shone bright through the greening buds of the aspens, peeking into the camp through the lingering mists just after sunrise. Giving a golden light whatever it touched, and warming the air with its rays.

Down in the valley, the sounds of activity were in full array already, as this was *rendezvous!* And for many, there was little time to make up for the months of loneliness, danger, and boredom.

Rendezvous was more than just a trade meeting between the trappers and traders from the companies. To a trapper, rendezvous is like Independence Day, New Year, Christmas and a birthday celebration all rolled up into one huge, sometimes month long event. There is gambling, and wrestling contests, boxing matches, and fights; as well as foot races, horse races, shooting competitions and knife and tomahawk throwing contests. And of course there were always the drinking contests.

One year "Big John" McGee brought a black bear on a chain into camp, and challenged all takers to wrestle his bear. For one dollar, a man had the chance to last five minutes wrestling the bear, and if he went the full five minutes, would gain a prize of a shiny new ten dollar gold piece. No one collected this prize, though many tried.

This year things were just starting to pick up as more and more crews began to come into camp from out in the mountains. Two Toes Brown had set up and marked out the camp only a week before but already the little town was in full swing as though it had been here for years.

The smell of coffee and bacon came to my nose, accompanied by the smell of frying onions and potatoes. *Potatoes??* I thought.

I rolled out of my blankets and wiped my eyes, before slipping into my moccasins, and getting up to start the day.

Tom and Samuel were sitting by the fire, cooking coffee in the coals and turning bacon as it sizzled in the pan over the fire. Long Walker was inspecting the new horses hooves, while everyone else was either still sleeping or had left camp already. Which of course didn't bother me a bit. I looked forward to the down time myself.

For no reason I could define, I had a woke in a particularly sour mood this morning, and was looking forward to a quiet cup of coffee to help remedy it. When I got closer to the fire, I noticed a new cast iron dutch oven in the coals with more piled on top. Apparently Tom had found himself a bigger oven for his biscuits, heavy as it was. I made no mention of it though as due to my mood I knew I would say the wrong thing.

"Where did you get potatoes Tom? And you got any eggs to go with that bacon?" I asked instead while I reached for a coffee cup to fill.

"You see any layin' hens around here?" Tom asked in response. " Taters came from down the Row, some Indian woman.. I'm gonna make gravy with the bacon grease to put on the biscuits." He informed me.

"There's eggs on the row if ya know where to look," I told him, "We had eggs for breakfast yesterday didn't we?"

Samuel broke in loudly as always, "Well ain't you the bloody prince of wales then?" and nodded at Tom "And him wanting eggs two days in a row now!"

"I forgot how good they are when ya cook em in the bacon grease." I told him as I got up and retrieved a small paper wrapped package from my tent. "It don't mean I got to have em every day." I handed the package to Tom, and added "Careful now there's only enough for the three of us, mare wouldn't give any more no matter how much I offered."

"You got to be joshin' me.." Tom was incredulous as he opened the paper, "Sure enough! Yer a sly one fer even six Silas! I'm surprised ya talked her outta that many!"

Samuel commented, "Maybe we should buy a couple o them hens and have eggs every day!"

"You would end up eatin' them chicken second day out!" Tom pointed out. "Indians would hear them chicken a cluckin' a mile a way let alone a rooster, and you would wake up with no eggs, no chickens, and no hair!"

"Im just gonna mix em all together, I don't have time to be cookin' individual here." Tom commented.

"What else ya got to do Tom?" I was not quite done with the sour of my mood yet, and sipped more coffee. Then added, "Ain't no trappin' to be done, no Indians to fight. What? You got an audience with the President or somethin'?"

Tom shook his head, "Nope, I'm gonna go get a couple of them pistols Cole was talkin about, if I can find em. If were goin' south, it be nice to have a pistol that shoots more than once."

I shot him a quick look to say no more on that subject, and he knew what I meant. "Besides," He added, "It weren't me that got up late for breakfast." He winked at me.

"Who's late? And *who brought the eggs?*" I reminded him.

"Fine, fried it is then," he surrendered, and dropped the subject. I felt a little bad for pulling rank on him like this, but I was in a sour mood and he had seen me like this before, and knew how to handle it.

He and Samuel talked of guns and fights they wished they would have had them in, while Tom finished cooking and we all ate. I heard little of this as my mind was on something far more important, and I had little room for much else.

The morning grew warmer with the rise of the sun over the mountain tops, and the mists retreated into nothingness for the day. As I ate I looked down over the little city in the valley, which was in full activity with the advent of the dry morning. One by one the rest of the men came to eat and get some coffee and start their day as well. Rendezvous was a special time and the men were eager to participate!

Several men off to one side of the miniature city of tents below were using a rope to measure out the distances for a firing range for the pistol and rifle shoot competitions. A group of loudly protesting Frenchmen were being escorted to a new campsite that was out of the line of fire.

Cook fires were in use all over the sprawling array of wall tents tipis, army style wedge tents and lean-to camps that made up the main encampment. Everywhere was the smell of food cooking, mixed with the wood smoke that drifted here and there, held on the slight breeze in a dull blue haze over the valley.

Somewhere at the other end of the tent city, a mule was braying, perhaps protesting being made to work on such a warm and pleasant morning.

It wasn't long after we finished eating, and were lighting our pipes, a shot rang out in the valley below, followed by a voice yelling an announcement out to the camp. In our camp in the trees we could not hear the actual words, but knew the voice to be Two Toes, and he was no doubt announcing the official start of trade on the Row, and the lighting of the council fire, which is where the administration of the little city met to discuss items of importance.

With the shot, Saul and Cole both came bounding out of their blankets in their long johns, rifles cocked and at the ready. Both had indulged in a bit too much whiskey the night before and had slept in, and awoke thinking the camp was under attack. Both were greatly relieved to find this was not true.

They both came to sit at the fire and nurse their hangovers with coffee and biscuits with gravy.

I stood and stretched my back, and told the men, "I think ill go down and scout out the row this morning, it'll do me good to talk a walk after such a fine breakfast. Thank you Tom."

Tom started to reply "No, thank you for the..." But I cut him off and winked, nodding at Saul and Cole, who caught on to something, they just didn't know what. "Shh..." I added while turning to go.

"Wait, what?" Saul asked Tom, but Tom just said "Oh nothing,... bacon?"

This morning I didn't ride down to the sprawling camp. I wanted to take my time and enjoy the morning. There is an amazing amount of birds that inhabit the Rockies, and it seemed this morning every species was represented here. I had always loved the spring songs of the birds, they always sounded joyful.

Activities were in full swing in the camp. Cook fires smoking, and people going about their intended business. In the lower end of the valley some Flathead were betting all comers to horse races.

Across the river in the Indian camps one could hear the music of the flutes they played in times of leisure or in ceremonies. Some sat on blankets outside their buffalo hide tipis and gambled.

Traders row was a hustle and bustle of activity. Men going all directions, from camp to camp, looking at the wares of the traders. Some to the camps of the Company buyers, where there were always heated discussions about the declining bounty on beaver especially.

I walked, almost strolled, down the row as I took it all in, as though I were walking through a busy market common back east. Though I will guarantee this was quite a bit more raucous. I was in no hurry, as most of the business I came to do was already done and now it was time to relax and take in the atmosphere of the rendezvous.

The amount and scale of the trade goods was staggering considering we were in the middle of nowhere in the wilds of such a raw land. Traders hawked their wares like the fishmongers in the sea towns in the east hoping to attract more business than their neighboring traders. This one selling axes and knives, powder ball and shot for all the firearms them men used to hunt these mountains. Others sold bolts of calico and tea cloth, wool socks long underwear and other such sundry. Others sold guns, while others yet sold dry goods or whiskey, whiskey being the number one sought after commodity in the camp.

I walked past tents full of furs and tanned leathers and hides, and others that sold pots and pans and tin cups and plates, coffee pots and wood and bone handled knives and forks. A little farther down, a black man was sitting by a blanket full of different traps, skinning a rabbit. On his three blankets were nearly fifty traps. I stopped for a moment and waited for the man to look up from his task before speaking.

When he did look up he instantly broke into a crooked grin and exclaimed "Silas! You old coon skinner you! Glad to see you still got your hair!"

"Buffalo Jack Jackson! You turn trader on us or you selling out and quittin'?" I asked. Jack set his rabbit down in a pot with another and stood to shake my hand.

"Neither," he answered, "Partner died and I don't need all them extra traps. Need the money though. Gonna go it alone this season, if I can't partner up here."

"Alone?" I found it surprising anyone would want to take the risk of working these lands alone. "Awful risky Jack you sure you wanna do that?"

"May have to," he nodded as he spoke. "Got no other choice ya know, not many in these mountains wanna partner with a nigger ya know!"

"All that don't apply out here Jack, not as far as I'm concerned." I told him.

"Oh but it do.. trust me it do.. almost as bad as Virginia when it comes to some." He put up a good point. "Oh hey I'm sorry, you want some coffee?" Jack pointed to a wood box off to the side. "Cups in the cook box, help yourself there." and stood to toss more wood on the fire.

Jack was a striking figure of a man, for any color. He stood well over six feet tall and Im sure weighed a good two hundred and thirty pounds. His buckskins were beaded with the work of a tribe I did not recognize, just that it was certainly done by someone with impeccable artistic ability and patience. He kept his head shaved, "Makes my hat fit better." He would say to those who asked why. And that hat was a well worn felt top hat once the high fashion across the east, but now tattered and misshaped, with a brightly beaded headband and what looked to be the feather of a red tailed hawk stuck in the hat band.

I took a cup from the box and poured myself some coffee and sat on a big rock next to the fire to drink it.

"Been cookin' a while, may be a bit thick. Got some sugar in the box too." He told me. He probably noticed the look on my face as I took a sip. It *was* strong.

"You always say that Jack but I suspect you just like burnt coffee!" I said. A few years ago Jack had been cook for a party of American Fur Company trappers in the Northwest Territories where we had met. The man could make a horse roast fall apart to the touch, and taste like one of them steaks served up in a New York restaurant. The men suspected he just didn't like making coffee because if any of them complained he would just shrug and tell them to go make it themselves. It seemed to work. Jack rarely had to make coffee after that.

"You shouldn't go it alone Jack," I said once we both sat with a cup of coffee, into his own Jack has poured a little whiskey too. "Its mighty risky out here. You ain't gonna last long alone what with all the Indians that are on the warpath against trappers."

"It ain't the same for a black man..." Jack answered. "... and it goes both ways. Them injuns don't see a white man it kinda confuses em a mite. They don't attack me on my own. Most jus' kinda watch and see what I'm gonna do."

I nodded, listening. "On the other hand," Jack continued, "I don't get many offers of partnership either. So if I have to, I go it alone. I can hep myself."

"Tell ya something Jack," I took another sip of the strong coffee before it got cold. "I lost a couple good men this season, and one more is goin' as now hes paid off, if I don't have to kill him. You sell your traps and come work with me. I got a new venture in mind and I can use a good man I can trust."

"I heard you was goin' off on some scoutin' trip this season. That musta panned out huh? Sure you ain't just lookin for some kinda lucky charm?"

"If it puts gold in yer pockets, what do you care?" I asked.

"Hmm, that word *do* put a whole new perspective on things don't it? You supply the horses and mules to haul camp, grub and supplies...." Jack scratched at his stubbly chin.

"And ten dollars a month in gold coin at the end of the season." I cut him off. "No trapping, cook and camp only." to which he nodded before he spoke.

"Ill want one more thing before I agree to sign on," he spoke slowly, as he always had when he was serious. "Well, no two. I want a good scatter gun, so's I can hunt birds time to time. Maybe some rabbits or other small game. I gets tired of venison and such all the time."

I nodded "Done! And the other thing?" I asked.

"I gotta bring my wife." Jack said quickly.

"Wife??" I couldn't believe my ears. "When did you go and get a wife?"

"Last year," He explained, "She a Navajo, but she was captured by some Apache for a time till she stole a horse and got away from 'em. She say she can't go back to her people now. She had a baby by one o them Apache and she thinks she wont be welcomed back by her family."

"Next your gonna tell me you got a baby with ya too?" I shook my head.

"No, no baby, she left the baby behind when she escaped too. Probably what kep 'em from comin' after her." Now his notion of goin' it "alone" made a lot more sense to me.

A little way down the row the sounds of many voices drifted up the hill. It sounded like someone was fighting and a crowd had gathered around to make bets and watch, which was another favorite distraction at a rendezvous. Gambling on just about anything from fights to horse races and shooting competitions.

"Alright, your wife can come too. Might be a nice change from having no women around." I agreed to his terms.

"You might regret you said that." Jack smiled "She don't like white men too much. And you'll have to warn the men. They're liable to wake up with a rattler in their bedroll some mornin' if'n they make her mad."

"I'll warn 'em sure," I agreed "but a couple of em already know what a squaw in camp can be like. Samuel once got hitched up with a Flathead woman. She was the kind that if ya made her mad she was liable to send pots and pans flying at your head." Jack laughed and nodded as I continued, "She even connected a few times. One of her victims, a man named Charlie, got hit so hard he never recovered. The last time I saw Charlie he was sitting in the back of a wagon with his head tilted to one side drooling on himself, unable to speak or recognize speech from anyone else. He just stared off into the air seeing... nothing."

A loud cheer went up down in the Hog Waller, signifying the end of the fight. From the sound of it several smaller fights had broken out over the decision of winner, as was often the case. I spent a good part of the day with Jack, remembering how much I had enjoyed his company in previous years.

I got up and tossed the grounds of my coffee into the fire, "Well I got more business to do before this day is done, You and your wife come to our camp and Ill introduce you to Tom and the men."

"I wouldn't expect no polite conversation from her Silas, I remind you she don't like white men too much." He said with a grin.

"Well the Apache been takin' scalps for years, and a couple of these boys know a man or two who died to Apache arrows. I'm sure it'll take a while for them to warm up to her too."

"She's Navajo Silas, she ain't Apache." He reminded me.

"All the same, how many years she lived Apache before she got away?" I asked.

"Twelve years, bet they ain't her people. She was a captive. A slave." Jackson replied "But I see your point."

"She don't have a gun does she?" I asked with a chuckle.

Jack just laughed and told me "No, no gun but look out if'n she got a rock in her hands, she deadly!"

"We will keep that in mind." I said as I shook his hand before going on about my business further down the row.

I casually wandered the camp for the rest of the day, listening for anyone who seemed to know Spanish. To my disappointment I heard nothing in any of the camps that remotely sounded like Spanish.

As luck would have it my friend Clay had a nice double barrel twelve guage flintlock fowling piece in his store on the row. He gave me an excellent price for it, and I took it with me and headed back to camp for the evening meal.

It was not quite dark yet, as the sun had set behind the mountains to the west, but there were still crimson and gold rays of light in the sky, and the clouds lit up a bright pink against the powder blue expanse. I was relieved to be going back to our camp as I did not like the hoards of people that constantly surround one in a large camp like this one. I never felt at ease, as at any time, one of them might flip their lid and boil over.

I got no more than halfway back to camp and David McNeil stepped out from behind a large pine.

"If not fer *you*, Mr Silas Horn, and your grand ideas, me brother would likely not be dead!" It was obvious from his speech that he was indeed still drunk. "I'm countin' you responsible for his early passin!"

He spoke calmly even though his face betrayed a deep rage within him. He smelled of whiskey, and his red rimmed eyes told of the length of his drunken state, and his face was the color of a ripe tomato.

"You're brother knew the risks same as anyone else David," I tossed him the little leather poke bag I had kept his and his brothers share in to him, and he let it bounce off his chest and drop to the ground. "There's the end of it now. You and your brothers share. Now be done with this, you don't need to hunt more trouble for yourself. Go take your brother home." I tried to be sensible, but David was having none of it.

"I'll take me brother home once *Im* done with *you!*" He sneered back at me and put his hand to the handle of his knife.

I knew this was coming so I leaned Long Stick against a tree along with the shotgun and my bags.

David drew his knife with a wicked grin. "Ill have yer guts on the ground soon *yer highness*!"

"No need to die David," I told him and drew my blade. I buried the tip into the tree and added, "You made the challenge, I choose the weapons and I choose fists"

David laughed and flipped his knife in the air, caught by the tip and flung it at me, narrowly missing my ear as I ducked to the side out of the way. He roared suddenly and grabbed for me thinking id be too distracted by his poor throw and catch me off guard and lunged at me with a left. I sidestepped and gave him a good hard uppercut into his sternum and he bent over gasping, and dropped to his knees. I stepped back in hopes that would be the end of it, but that didn't happen.

He slipped once before he was able to regain his feet in the slippery conditions, but was not deterred. He came swinging again, this time a desperate wide right roundhouse meant to end the fight in one blow, but wasn't fast enough and I hit him in his wind again. This time he rushed forward and shoved with both fists under my chin while stepping on my foot, and tried to shove me over backward.

As I regained my balance he was able to land a solid right to my left temple that made stars appear in my vision for a moment. Then a flash of lightning as he caught me immediately after with a left to the other side of my head. I lowered my head and put a jab between his eyes and broke his nose.

David stumbled backwards, spitting blood and wiping it from his face. He then dove at me and tried knocking me off my feet backwards, which is a move I was expecting, and I rolled backward to the ground and planted a foot in his gut, and rolled him over top of me onto the ground behind me. I beat him to his feet by only an instant, but it was enough.

David tried for a punch to my groin, but I stepped out of the way just in time, and the blow landed on my hip. I gave him a good stiff right to his left eye, cutting his brow instantly and pouring blood into his eye. Immediately I took his head in both hands and brought it down as I brought up my knee to meet it, and he went down.

I dropped down on top of him and hit him with a left, and a right, and another left, until his head no longer offered any resistance and he lay limp. I stood slowly gasping for air and looked down at him moaning like a sick calf and trying to roll over to get up.

"You.. should a... waited till... ya weren't drunk!" the words came out of me between gasping for breaths of air. I took up the sack with his coin and dropped it beside his head. "I put extra in there to help get your brother back to Ioway country. And the horses you and your brother used are now yours.. Don't let me see you again! The next time you come at me with a knife. I'll kill you!" I gathered my things and left him laying there in the mud bleeding. But I had no doubt I would see him again. Some people just cant let things go. And the Irish especially!

When I got back to camp several of the men were sitting around the fire. Tom cooking some sourdough bread in his new dutch oven, to go with the haunch of venison roasting over the fire.

There was a pot of something hanging over the fire emitting steam from its lid and smelled like some kind of stew.

Buffalo Jack was sitting off to one side with a little whisp of a girl dressed in buckskins, hunting shirt and a broad black hat a bit too big for her. Due to her dress and short hair I might have mistaken her for a boy or a small man.

"I see you got to meet the men Jack," I said as I sat close to them after putting my gear in my camp. "Here's that shotgun, and powder and shot for it, as I promised." He took the weapon from me and looked it over.

"Looks like it will do the deed for shore!" He said slowly. "This better than I asked for, I never had one with two barrels before! I surely thank you!"

"You never did tell me your woman's name Jack. What do we call her?" I realized I had not asked him before.

"Well I can't say her name, so's I jus call her Jill. Ya know like that old child story "Jack and Jill go up dat hill..."

"That *does* make sense," I admitted with a chuckle, "Does she speak English?"

"I speak it, Jack teach me." Jill answered up for herself.

"Welcome Jill, It is nice to meet you." I said to her, she just snorted in contempt.

"I told ye she don't like white men, I didn't lie." Jack smiled at me while he spoke.

"You did not lie." I smiled back, and turned to leave them to their own.

While the men ate, and talked of their day and passed the whiskey jug, Tom and I took Paul McVeigh, and Samuel aside for a bit of a planning discussion. We decided that if we were going to reorganize the two twenty man crews and have one head south with me and Tom, each man was going to have to choose for himself which crew he wanted to be a part of. For those who went with me there would be new rules in dealing with the natives of the lower mountains.

This was the first time I told anyone but Tom of the existence of the Spanish map. After this talk it was agreed that we four would head south following the map, and the rest of the men would choose a new leader to remain in the northern mountains or the northwest territories.

But there was time. For the next few days, it was time to relax and drink in the warmer temperatures and enjoy the comradeship of the rendezvous. The men had been looking forward to it for months. There was time to discuss plans further once the allure of the rendezvous began to wear off and the men were ready to go back to work.

Long Walker stepped from the shadows when the meeting broke up and told me "Red Hair David take three ponies and leave. Head south on the trail we come here on. I think he go to find his brother again."

"Three horses. I gave him two." I took a sip of the whiskey jug and wiped the runoff from my beard, then handed it to Cole to pass on. "It is worth the extra to see him go! Hopefully that will be the last time we see him! But I don't think it will be." I added

Long nodded and said softly "He will come back. He wants to kill you."

Behind us the men passed the jug and began singing and telling jokes and tall tales.

"I want you to go looking for someone while we finish up our business here." I told Long. "I need someone who can read Spanish and speak English, who can be trusted with secrets. I know there are still settlements of Spanish and Mexicans in the south. I want you to go find someone we can trust, and meet us at the White river in four weeks."

Long nodded as he listened. I went on to add "If you do not find someone in that time we will join up there and you can guide us to villages to look into."

Long replied, "I know the villages, it is where my people are too. I will find someone there." And turned and left. He didn't like Rendezvous. He preferred to be alone on a trail. And I didn't blame him.

Chapter 11

Stone Bear was angry this morning. His back hurt from sleeping wrong, and his scar was bothering him terribly this morning. It was the weather. His scar always itched and ached when the weather was changing. This morning it ached more than it itched, which made him feel particularly grumpy. Something he had eaten had turned everything in his bowels to liquid, and gave him cramps in his belly, and that was not helping either.

He threw a piece of wood into the fire and watched the sparks float up and out of the smoke flaps of his lodge. He had not slept well after Young Bear, his son, had come to tell him the night before that Black Coyote had convinced about thirty of the warriors to go again in search of the white men invading their mountains.

Stone Bear knew that Black Coyote was only bent on revenge, and it had turned his heart cold. He was no longer rational, and instead was intent on making war. *How can he be so insolent and stubborn?* He thought. Didn't he know Stone Bear was the head of the warrior society now and had said nothing of raiding parties?

It was evident to all that Black Coyote had no respect for the words of White Medicine Bear, but to go on the war path over one trespassing white man was a waste of time. There were more important things happening in the lower valley.

It was reported that the white men had begun to build a fort on the great river not far from the adobe lodges. It seemed these whites wanted to trade for the furs not to come and take them. Perhaps White Medicine Bear could go with a scouting party when he returned, to see the intentions of these whites.

"Walks With Ghosts wishes to speak to you husband." Paints Her Face said as she entered the tipi. "He is in his lodge." she added as she set her basket of berries in its place to the side and sat in her place.

Stone Bear grunted his reply and stood and left to go find out what the medicine man wanted. Didn't he know this was not a good time?

Walks with Ghost had his lodge on the other side of the camp. Along the way he passed the homes of his people. People who respected him and those he in turn respected and loved. He was responsible for keeping the people protected and safe from the dangers that were ever present in their lives.

Stone Bear walked past where Two Crows sat painting a deerskin. He would have to go back and look at what he painted when he was done. It may be significant.

Two Crows had once painted a puma killing a horse, and later that day one of the boys who guard the pony head came to report a puma had killed a new foal and drug it off into the woods. Ever since then the people were very interested in what Two Crows painted.

When he got to the lodge of Walks With Ghosts, Stone Bear found the old medicine man at his outside fire peeling a little green snake. He waited while the old man threw the skin of the snake into the fire to see which way it curled before it burned. The skin curled inside out and the shaman poked the skin with a stick, and the skin stuck and curled around the stick and burst into flames. The old man hissed and threw the stick into the fire along with the body of the snake and laid a green branch of a pine over it.

When the thick white smoke started he leaned forward and put his face into the smoke and sniffed long. The old man leaned back with a look of surprise on his face. He should have sneezed from the smoke but he didn't, and this puzzled him. He stood up with a confused look on his face, as he always looked until he spoke. Suddenly he turned and went inside his lodge and left the entry flap open behind him.

Stone Bear followed him inside, and went around the fire to the guest spot by the old man. He sat and waited for the old man to speak.

"A time of change is coming for the people." The old man began, "Many Crow people will die. The people will be given a new land on which to live. The way of the warrior is coming to an end and a new time will come where the people will have to learn a new way to live."

Stone Bear watched the old man, seated on his puma skin behind the fire. The firelight dance off the bear claw necklace around his neck. And from the silver concho that held the eagle feather to his black hair-pipe breast plate decorated with red beads.

The medicine mans skin looked like the rawhide of a buffalo that had been left to dry in the sun without being stretched. Wrinkled with deep canyons in the skin of his forehead and face... pockmarked from an illness he had suffered as a boy. But the firelight glinted in his dark eyes and told of a wisdom behind them.

Stone Bear could no longer hold his question. "What change. When will this change come?"

"The one who brings change is coming soon." was the old mans cryptic reply. He fell silent again and Stone Bear waited for him to speak again as it was not wise to press a Medicine Man too quickly.

After a pause Walks With Ghosts threw some sacred sage into the fire and turned and took out his pipe. It was already loaded as was his habit and he put the stone bowl into the fire to light it. As he smoked for a moment he rocked back and forth and hummed a little tune to himself. He then held the bowl close to his face and wafted the smoke into his face and over his head three times before exhaling the smoke.

He then handed the pipe to Stone Bear who repeated the same ritual. Stone Bear breathed his lung full of smoke to the sky and handed the pipe back to the old man as he began to speak.

"A time is coming when the Apsaalooke people will move far away from this land. There will be sickness and many people will not have enough to eat." The old man looked straight ahead but his vision was far away as he spoke. "The Maker of All Life has shown me that this must happen, so that the sick and the weak will die, to make the people stronger in the time to come."

Stone Bear began to feel unease creep into his heart.

The old man went on, "These things must be endure for the welfare of the people. White Medicine Bear also has had this vision. He tell of the white people who live in the ground and only come out at night. He tells of the blue men on war horses. The blue men will make war on the People all the way to the big salty lake and drive them north to Kanata to live along side their enemies the Blackfeet."

Stone Bear shuddered at this thought, but let the old man go on.

"Already we have heard of this happening in the east, with Cherokee, Creek, Tuscarora, Sauk And Fox, and many others forced to give up their homes. And so must we as well, or there will be only suffering and sickness, misery and death for the people until there are no more Apsaalooke left."

Walks with Ghosts fell silent, and Stone Bear waited politely for a time to make sure the old man was finished speaking his vision before he spoke.

The old mans pipe was strong and Stone Bear spoke slowly to make sure he was saying the right words. "Many of our people will not accept this change. Those like Black Coyote and Broken Nose will always fight. For them it is what is right. They will raid the Ute and the Blackfeet, the Flathead and the Cheyenne as we always have. And they will kill the whites who come to take Apsaalooke lands.

They see the whites have no honor and are only here driven by greed to take what they want. Did not we hear they have taken women from the Blackfeet in the north? How can one reason with those who are not sane?"

Stone Bear paused for a moment to let his head clear a moment before going on, Walks With Ghosts pipe had always had strong smoke and made his head feel clouded. "Many people are hard to lead away from how they have always lived. The People are afraid of changes for to them change means death. They would rather die fighting for the old ways to continue than be forced to change to a new way they do not understand."

Walks with Ghosts nodded, and replied "I do not envy you your position. I can see which way a snakeskin curls in the fire. I can see plainly which way the crow turns his head when he calls. But you must look and see what is in their hearts. You must tell them what they do not want to hear. It is a dangerous position to be in."

"Black Coyote thinks he should be leader of all warriors. Some of the young men believe in him and his words. He does what he wishes and not what is best for the people." Stone Bear spoke solemnly while looking into the fire. "I think this will make life very hard for the People."

Stone Bear also wished the people could continue living as they always had, but also saw wisdom in the vision of White Medicine Bear and Walks With Ghosts. "I will speak with White Medicine Bear again."

Stone Bear felt a familiar twisting in his belly indicating he needed to find a place quickly to empty his bowels, yet again. He got up to leave but the old man took hold of his arm and stopped him. "A warrior comes, one who can be in two places at the same time. His medicine is strong. He will come to live in the valley of the bear. His grandsons will be your great grandsons. He will signal the sun to rise on a new way for the people. Do not fear the one who comes."

Stone Bear puzzled at these words as he stepped back out into the daylight. He would have to think long on the words of the medicine man. But first. . .

Chapter 13

Long Walker enjoyed the time of solitude when he was on a scout. It was when he felt most in tune with his mind, and could be one with the land and animals. It was something he had learned when he was a boy, to enjoy the silence.

Silas had said to find someone who can read the Spanish words on the map. Someone who could be trusted, and Long Walker could only think of ONE that he would trust with such and important matter. The hope that he could find him or that he was even still alive, or hadn't been run out by the Apache or the Kiowa and Comanche, was only what was on the surface in his mind. Espinoza had been kind to him in the seasons following his exile from his band of Ute. Espinoza could be trusted.

It was a long journey to the valley that Espinoza lived in with his woman and children, so Long was mounted with a pack horse for supplies as he must travel quickly in order to meet back with Silas at the White River in one moons time.

He was traveling in very familiar country now, as these ranges in the Colorado territory were where he had lived for many years when he had to leave his people. Not only was he in familiar territory but he was among tribes that were friendly to him, if not to his people. The Cheyenne had fought his people over the mountain hunting grounds for ages, as well as the Comanche and the Kiowa.

A band of Cheyenne had befriended him at one time when they found him wandering alone in a high mountain valley. He knew of their summer camps in the mountains and would be able to find shelter there, and perhaps game as well.

It was then that he was shown the trail that follows the peaks of the mountain ranges, that the people had been using since the time of their grandfathers grandfathers. By using the high mountain trail, he could avoid most of the unfriendly tribes until he got to more friendly country in the south.

An eagle screamed above his head and he reigned in his horse to watch it for a moment. The eagle flew in high circles almost floating on the breeze with no effort. Long recognized this as the bird hunting and disregarded it.

Everything that happens around a human in the wild places happens for a reason. Whether it be the chatter of a squirrel or the cries of the birds, one must know them all and know what they mean if one is to remain alive while traveling alone, especially on the steep dangerous trails at this high elevation.

For days now he had seen no other human on the trail, it seemed as though he was the only one in this region of the mountains. But appearance are rarely what they seem to be, so he rode on with caution.

At night he made camps in the upper treeline where there was game, and wood for the fire. This high up in the mountains one could freeze even in the summer if he wasn't careful.

Long Walker had been with Silas Horn for six years now, after meeting him on a trail in Ute-ah. Silas was having some difficulty in communicating with a few Flathead that had accused him of trespassing on their hunting ground and poaching game. Long Walker came upon the group just as the Flathead were about to attack and had diffused the situation through Indian hand sign.

It was once the Flathead were convinced that Silas and his men were merely passing through the area, as even many warring tribes do on the big rivers, that Silas realized Long Walker had saved his life and the lives of his men. He asked Long if he would like to sign on with the expedition as a guide and scout. Long had been a lone wanderer for many years at this point, and welcomed the chance to act as scout for Silas.

Silas always treated him as equal when other whites always acted like Indians were inferior to whites. Long Walker appreciated this and even began to call Silas a brother.

Today as he rode, he had the uneasy feeling someone was watching him. He had these feelings all the time and knew that that 'someone' may not necessarily human. He tuned his ears more closely to the sounds around him as he rode.

This part of the trail was interspersed with the twisted high mountain pines and junipers that were hardy enough to survive the harsh environment. These were also excellent places for predators to conceal themselves looking for prey. Puma, and Bear, and Wolf, all came to these places in the summers. They would hunt the elk herds during the season they dropped their calves.

Soon a familiar scent came to his nose and his sense of being watched began to make more sense. The stink of brown bear came to his nose the same time it did to that of his horses, and they began to show signs of fear.

Long spoke low and soft to them and it calmed them enough to continue to move forward. The trail opened up to a vast rock slide. The trail wound back and forth up and down the mountain, picking places where the ground was solid. Everything else was shale that if one was to take one wrong step he would tumble to his death and be immediately covered by the landslide he had caused.

The trail was only a few hand widths wide, enough for a horse and rider but not much else. He would have to ride carefully and lead his pack horse on a longer lead so it could follow behind in single line.

About halfway across the steeply slanted field of loose rock he came to a rise in the trail and soon saw the source of the smell and uneasy feeling. A sow and her two cubs were uphill from the trail among the rocks. Down the mountain there were two more sows with one cub each. If they saw Long Walker or his horses they didn't seem to care. They were busy feeding on the moths that live there among the rocks.

The bears of the big mountains had learned this precious source of ready food among the rocks at the beginning of time, and Long knew that right now was the perfect time to slowly continue his path onward and the chances were the bears were all too busy gorging themselves on the moths, to care that he was in their territory and attack.

The thing he worried about the most was that in feeding on the moths in the rocks the bears would overturn them and cause a landslide that would be the end of Long Walker and his horses. Then *surely* they would become a meal for the bears.

Now and then a little slide would start and put a flutter in Long Walkers belly, but most just tumbled or rolled a little way, causing a big cloud of dust to blow away in the wind.

As he steadily rode on south, he also noticed some mountain sheep farther off in the distance.

Where there were sheep in these mountains, there were Puma. He must keep his eyes open and aware at every turn now. There were high country predators here that would have no problem making a meal of him or his horses.

Just about the time he was beyond where the grizzlies fed among the rocks, everything changed in the blink of an eye. He heard a the roar of a big boar grizzly from behind him and up the mountain and the response of the sow warning the big male to stay away. This was a sound he knew well, and also knew what it meant.

It meant there was about to be a battle and he and his horses were *now* in the perfect position to be directly in the path of the rock slide that would certainly be the end result of a battle between the great bears of the mountain.

Even though the trail was rocky and thin, he had no choice but to pick up the pace and urge his horses into a trot, to gain some distance between them and the destruction that was about to happen in their path.

Just as he was about to get off the slide area into the treeline on the other side the battle erupted in earnest. The roaring of the huge bears came to his ears and frightened his horses to the point he almost could not control them. But with some effort was able to calm them enough to ride, now at a canter, further down the trail into the relative safety of the trees.

The sound of a great rock slide came to his ears as he slowed his pace again, and he turned to look at the trail behind him. Sure enough a big cloud of dust billowed up from the mountain, as the battle between the ferocious beasts ensued. He was just able to catch sight of the two bears, locked in each others grip, tumble down the mountain across the path where he and his horses had just been.

He took the time to calm his breath, and the nerves of his horses, before continuing. A dark cloud had begun to form over the peaks of the mountains, and he was going to have to find shelter soon, before the storm began.

He began looking for an outcropping or shallow cave to use for protection from the storm. It was not long after the lightning and thunder began, that he found what he was looking for, an over hang of rock large enough for he and his horses to shelter and ride out the storm. The storms usually didn't last too long in these mountains, but they were fierce.

He dismounted and hobbled his horses so they wouldn't run off in the storm, and made camp.

There was probably a better place to make camp, but not any place close enough, so this would have to do.

Chapter 14

Once again Bolt started to buck and crow-hop as soon as I stepped into the saddle. We had been taking a little time to get the new horses attuned to being ridden by white men. Most had not been ridden much, and none had ever worn a saddle before so the going was tough.

The big stallion's breath came in puffs of steam in the chilly mountain morning air as he tried to buck me off his back. We had done this same dance every morning for a few days, and though he was hard headed, he was learning. Slowly.

This morning though, he finally decided he was not going to be able to buck me off, and started to calm some. He still side stepped, pranced, and reared a bit. He tossed his head trying to get rid of the bit in his mouth, but finding he was unsuccessful, eventually came to a standstill.

Bold stood shivering, and slightly tossing his head, but he stood. I reigned him around to the right and he followed the reigns, then to the left and he changed direction as though he had been ridden all his life. I liked the fact that he was still half wild and full of spirit. Those things would serve me well in the wild places we worked and lived in.

A wild horse can sense danger long before a human can. I disagreed with the term 'breaking' a horse...I didn't want a broken horse.. I wanted a trained horse with a wild spirit, and Bolt was just that.

When he gave in and decided I want going to hurt him, only ask to ride him, he snorted his acceptance of me as his rider, and began to walk in any direction I chose, without complaint or a fight. Once he stopped shivering at my touch, and stood still and calm I dismounted.

"You'll get it yet, boy." I said patting him on his neck.

The morning was just turning from gray dull foggy light to having a hint of orange with the coming of the sun when I got him rubbed down and picketed with the others again.

My partner Paul McVeigh had coffee going over the fire when I got into camp, and was sitting with Tom so I took my cup out of my pack and poured myself a cup of Paul version of coffee. If I were to give my honest opinion though I would say it was river mud.

"Leave it to you Silas to pick a stallion to ride!" Paul remarked, "I was watchin' for a bit there and I swear he's tryin to kill ya as much as buck ya off!"

"You would too if Silas climbed on yer back every mornin' before breakfast!" Tom interjected.

I sat on a stump out of the reach of the smoke to sip my coffee. "The Spanish done it for centuries, Indians too, as long as they've had horses. The Nez Perce and some other tribes break em by leading them into a small lake or pond before they get on the first time.." I told them of the time I had seen it myself in the Northwest Territory. "Its a bit of a rougher ride, and ya got to think one step ahead of him all the time, but in my opinion all that is worth it."

"Hell even gelded these are the best mountain horses I've seen yet," Paul exclaimed. "Big in the front, big in the back, thick in the middle. Smooth as silk up or down hill."

"Between all of us, I'd say we got the best string of horses for these mountains over any other party." Samuel joined the conversation from behind a tree where he was relieving himself. Then came back to the fire smoothing his kilt and adjusted his pistol in his belt before he sat. "Damn near cleaned out Ol Dick as well!"

Tom nodded "I agree, Ol Dicks gonna have to bring more horses next rendezvous. I heard he had only the ones he rode in on by the time rendezvous was over."

"Well, since all the crew leaders are here, we may as well get this out of the way now." I stood up and reached for one of Toms biscuits while I talked. "Some of you have a hard decision to make." I tuned and looked at the six men I would now trust with the truth of this years excursion.

"I want to do things a little different this year. I have come into possession of a map that shows the ranges of mountains from here down to Mexico territory. The problem is none of us here can read Spanish. I sent Long Walker south to go look for a man he says he knows that can help."

"Where did you come across a *map??*" Cole interrupted, "I thought this was all un-mapped territory. I only ever seen hand drawn maps from old trappers now and then, but a map of the whole range??"

"Remember the cave I told you about, where I healed up last winter before we crossed paths again?" I went on as they all nodded "I found not only a cache of supplies that looked like it was left y the Spanish a hundred years ago, but also found some mining equipment and rock samples that I *know* are too modern to be from the same time."

"SO THIS is what you and Tom been a whisperin' about the last couple weeks is it?" Samuel seemed fully interested now.."Mining equipment you say? Rock samples, ye say..." His voice drifted off in thought as he scratched at his beard.

I went on. "You have all noticed that a few of the pack horses are pretty heavily loaded for this early in the season. Those packs are loaded with trade goods for the Indians. I want to try to make friends in the tribes to the south, for from what I hear they are formidable as enemies."

"I get the feeling Im not gonna like this next part Silas but do, go on. I am intrigued." Samuel commented.

"We are not going to sneak around and try to work under the noses of the Indians anymore. I learned last year they are pretty aggressive about they're territory here, and not so forgiving as those we know from up in the Northwest. Along with this goes something else. *If we DO* get into skirmishes with any of the tribes, we WILL NOT practice taking scalps any longer! Any who choose to come with me will drop that habit here and now. It is a savage practice and incites men to murder." I paused a moment for this idea to sink in.

Saul and Cole were both looking at each other as if in silent conversation as they often did. Samuel seemed deep in thought as he had adopted this practice back in the war, as many men did. The others seemed to be waiting for me to continue so I went on.

"Those who cannot abide this new rule can go north with Saul, and a party of men who wish to do things as they always have. I cannot make anyone do anything, even when we are well on this mission, so each man must make his own choice now, before we go any further." I paused again and finished my coffee and tossed the dregs into the fire.

"Well now," Tom spoke first "I suppose its come down to figuring out how many men we WILL have on this trip. Askin' men to change is like asking the sky to change color."

"My crew all want to go north again, all in all fourteen men to go with Saul, Cole? You goin too?" Paul asked.

"I think the idea of changing from trapping to trading seems like a great idea to me," Cole responded "I'm tired of wading in them frozen streams all day every day, I'm in!" He looked at Saul and Saul just nodded, he had had a feeling Cole would go for *new* adventures. It was just his way.

"You still comin' with us this Paul?" Tom asked.

"Oh yeah I'm in.. Im real curious about this map and the link to mining equipment. Might be somethin' to that I don't wanna miss out on" Paul stated, then went on to say "I got damn tired of mining coal before the army, but I don't think coal would be a reason for the Spanish to have a map, especially marked with location markers like you described Silas, Oh yes I'm in. And I know Mato Sapa will stand with my decision as well, when he gets back from his hunt."

By the end of the vote, Andre LaFleur, Adam Forsythe, Monty the Mute as some now called him, all accepted the new rules, with the promise of new adventure along with Myself, Paul McVeigh Cole Stevens, Tom Sweet, Buffalo Jack and his woman all signed on for the trip south.

"Andre, I noticed a couple more men at your fire this morning, did you pick up some stragglers at rendezvous?" Tom asked.

"Men I trust, and who can be trusted." He replied. "Ill lay out the rules of this trip to them and let them make their choices and get back to you at first light."

"Good enough" I broke in. Tom nodded his agreement

"Well!" Cole exclaimed, "Always did wanna die in a new land I never seen, I guess this is as good a chance as any!"

"Good possibility of it." I replied "From what I hear of the tribes down south from Long Walker, they are not to be fooled with and as likely to kill you as look at you if they don't like your look."

"And ye want us to do it all without any scalpin, truly?" Samuel was the last to speak on the subject. "I am truly intrigued Silas, I'll go with ye, and I will have Standing Fox with me as well, he is with Mato Sapa on the hunt."

"When ya wanna head out? This here rendezvous is losin' its allure with every day now." Paul asked.

Im thinking two days from now, when Mato Sapa is back with Standing Fox." I replied. "Tom and I are gonna go scout out a trail to start on tomorrow. That gives plenty of time for each man to finish up his business here and get organized for a long trip."

Everyone agreed to this time frame, and the conversation ended, and the men fell to eating breakfast which Tom and Saul had been preparing while we had our discussion.

Breakfast consisted of bacon and beans, cornbread with honey Standing Fox had found, along with Toms sourdough biscuits and eggs bought from Mare. She was a little unhappy with giving over so many, until Tom produced a gold nugget from is vest pocket to give her. She had little use for coin, but was very happy to accept the gold.

The men ate leisurely, enjoying the warming temperatures as the fog lifted and gave way to golden rays of sunshine breaking over the peaks of the mountains to the east of us. These were lazy moments, too far between, and too few... hard earned moments of rest and relaxation to sit by a fire and sip coffee, smoke a pipe and enjoy the conversation of men.

A trappers life is mostly a solitary one, so mountain men are alone for long periods of time during the trapping season. Time spent in the company of other men at rendezvous was to be savored. A few, even when given the chance to socialize, still prefer the quiet of the solitude here in the mountains. Most though relish the time spent in the company of other men, for the know that soon they will be knee deep in some frozen pond working alone again with nothing but his own mind for conversation. And believe me trying to carry on a conversation with yourself is a lot harder than it sounds! And at the very least it gets very boring!

Today though I wished for the solitude. I needed to be alone with my thoughts and prepare myself for this new venture into unknown lands. After breakfast, and a third cup of coffee, I grabbed up some leftover bacon and a biscuit, and put them in my saddle bag. As I tied it to my saddle I spoke softly to Bolt.

"Time to get things right between us boy, we got a lot of territory to cover and id rather we do it as friends." I rubbed him down and saddled him while the conversation of the men went on behind me. But I paid no attention to the voices, I was focused on Bolt. Today would be the day we would come to an agreement, or part ways. And the decision was to be his to make.

"Time to go for a ride, boy, tomorrow we go to work." I said softly as I stepped into the saddle slowly, giving him time to get used to my weight, and giving me time to assess his reaction.

Surprisingly he stood stock still and let me mount with only the slightest of a shudder of his flanks. And for that matter that could have been because of a horse fly bite. As I settled into the saddle I felt him tense a little, and then almost immediately relax. *'whew, that went well."*

I thought, though I still expected at any moment for him to launch into bucking again like every other time I had gotten on him.

Once he relaxed I patted him on his neck and squeezed his sides slightly and clicked at him with my tongue, and he stepped out as if he had done it all his life. I reigned him up hill towards the mountain. I pointed him at a notch between two peaks, which was where the start of our journey south would begin and urged him into a canter.

It didn't take long before I was quite a ways from camp, and the din of the rendezvous and felt like I could hear my own thoughts again.

Fast Hare and Bird Hunter watched as the white trappers turned south on the high mountain trail the ancient ones made, and left a marker for Black Coyote and the rest of the warriors to follow when they caught up. Both were surprised that these whites even knew about the high trail, as even some of the wider ranging tribes didn't use them. It was a hard trail, but a quicker route to the south lands.

"They go to the land of the Tsehesenetsestotse." Fast Hare said to his friend. "Black Coyote must hurry if we are going to catch them before they are out of Apsaalooke land."

"Black Coyote also wants this," Bird Hunter responded, "I do not think he wants to fight the Tsehesenetsestotse with so few warriors. I do not feel this is a good thing. We will need to make strong medicine to make war on so many white, especially if the make it into the land of Tsehesenetsestotse."

"The Tsehesenetsestotse are at war with the Numunuu." Fast Hare noted, "I would not wish to walk into a battle with both. We would need every warrior in the village."

"I believe you are right," Bird Hunter agrees, "But I also believe in the words of Black Coyote, these whites should not be allowed to come and take what they wish any longer. That is why I have come, whether the raid goes well or not, is not in my hands to decide."

Fast Hare jumped down from the boulder he had been using as a lookout, and mounted his pony. "We will go tell the others, and send Short Wolf back to Black Coyote and tell him what we have seen."

. . . .

BLACK COYOTE LEAPT onto his buckskin pony lifted his lance and whooped for all to hear then shouted his challenge to the warriors gathered around. "I AM BLACK COYOTE! Who will come and hunt the whites with me?? Who will stand for the People and protect them from the invasion of the whites? I AM BLACK COYOTE! APSAALOOKE WARRIOR! AND I AM NOT AFRAID! I WILL MAKE WAR! WHO WILL RIDE WITH ME??"

The shouts and war whoops of nearly forty warriors answered him and all began to raise their weapons and circle their horses, getting ready to go on the war trail.

Each warrior had painted his face for war. Each wore their war shirts, decorated with their medicine that protected them in battle, and decorated their battle ponies for protection from the bullets of the whites. Once the war cries died down, the warriors all turned at once, as a flock of birds, and fell in line with Black Coyote leading the way, riding towards the high mountain trail that would take them through the mountain to the other side, where the gathering of whites was held.

• • • •

FAR TO THE SOUTH, LONG Walker rode across the White River at a slow crossing. And entered the eastern regions of the land of his people the Ute. Memories came to him as he rode. Though it had been many winters since he had seen these lands, his eyes recognized them as they did before.

He felt no emotion other than a sense of being at home. These mountains were where his people would hunt buffalo, elk and antelope in summers. He was seven days ride from the little village where Espinoza lived, if he still lived.

A sound came to his ears, and he reigned his horse to a stand still listening. Soon the sound was loud enough to hear; the sound of horses on the rocky trail in front of him. Quickly Long Walker dismounted and led his horses into a small stand of junipers and lodge pole pines thick enough to conceal them, and waited to see who it was that was coming down the trail towards him.

Soon he heard voices, and identified their language as Arapaho. The Ute had never had much problem with Arapaho, but Long wasn't taking chances on this trip. When the small group of Arapaho came to where his trail ended and he had gone into the trees, they stopped for a moment to inspect the tracks.

The trail was rocky and Long was sure they would not find any tracks that would identify him as Ute, or even human. Many time the tracks of elk looked much the same as the tracks of horse on these rocky mountain trails.

A short discussion took place among the Arapaho, and after some argument it seemed, the decided the tracks meant nothing and decided to go on north.

None of the warriors were painted for war and their ponies were plain, and Long Walker decided that this must be a hunting party sent into the high lands for elk, which took to the high country in the springs and summers to graze on the lush grasses and shrubs that grew there.

Looking at his surroundings, Long decided this was good a place as any to camp for the night, and avoid making any sign of his presence visible to any Arapaho that decided to check their back trail.

He waited until almost sundown before he took off his horses' saddle and packs, and make a small camp for the night. He would have no fire tonight, as there may be others on the trail that would see, and come to investigate who was in these mountains. He was Ute and this was the land of his people, but he was a stranger now, and would be treated as a stranger by any he would meet on the trail.

After the sun set, only when he heard the call of an owl did he relax. He would have to be more careful as he continued. This was a close call and although he did not fear that a chance meeting would become a fight, he did not wish to casually let others in the area know of his presence either.

There was always a chance that he may run into a party of Apache or Kiowa even this far north pf the high desert plains where they lived and hunted. And there was always the risk that the Comanche would catch him alone. The Comanche, or their allies the Kiowa, would surely torture him for fun as they always had when they captured an enemy alone and helpless.

Perhaps he should begin to travel at night, and rest during the day. This would better hide his movements and allow him to traverse the country in secret better.

All through the night and into the next day, Long saw nor heard any sign of anyone on the trail. This assured him the Arapaho had not detected him as they passed, and that he would be free to continue his journey south with the coming of darkness.

As fate would have it, when the darkness came the moon shone brightly, almost full, on his trail.

This was when he also made the decision to take the lower hills trail, which provided much better cover for him to make his way unseen.

After three days traveling at night, Long Walker began to see signs of the pueblo people, and their neighbors the Mexican/Spanish settlers that remained after the armies of Spain left the land to the Indians.

It was still best to travel at night to remain undetected, and now he could use the landscape of the high desert plain to guide him to the village where he last knew Espinoza to live.

Along the trail one day some movement caught his eye. He looked closer at one of the buttes in the not too far distance and saw white dots that indicated to him he was in the land of the sheep eaters, and knew he was getting close to his destination. The people in these lands had never been known to be warlike. They would defend themselves fiercely, but were not known to be enemies to anyone. Their only enemy was the Spanish that enslaved them, and the Mexicans who treated them as if they were a lower class of people.

In two more days ride, he came to the village where he remembered Espinoza to live, and made a small camp out of town. It would do well for him to picket the horses not far out of the little pueblo, and walk to the home of Espinoza, like the Pueblo people walked, in order to seem more a part of the community and may not be questioned as to his purpose there.

As luck would have it, Espinoza did still live in the same village and also remembered Long Walker well. He was married now, with children, and lived a simple life in a sleepy little Mexican settlement named Taos.

With the promise of gold in payment Espinoza readily agreed to go with Long Walker, and help translate the Spanish Map.

Amid the tears of his wife Marian, Espinoza accompanied Long Walker back to his camp the next day, mounted on his mule, to begin the days-long ride back to the White River to meet Silas and his men.

Chapter 16

All in all, twenty seven men, and one woman, traveled with Tom, Paul and I on this new excursion to the south. It had now been weeks of hard riding in unforgiving territory, following this high mountain trail into unfamiliar territory before we came to the White River where we were to meet Long Walker.

Once we came down from the high mountain trail and into the lower lands, in order to make the going a bit easier, I had taken an idea from the Indians of the area, and had the men fashion travois' to pull behind the horses. The horses seemed to appreciate the more familiar hitch, instead of using them as pack horses, and they seemed to be more cooperative. This also saved time in loading and unloading them at each camp along the way.

It is a fool who cannot adapt and must make his surroundings fit him, instead of fitting into his surroundings. The more we appeared to be a band of Indians from a distance the better.

When we got to the easy crossing Long Walker had described to us, we made camp and waited for Long Walker to join us. .

Thirty people is a lot to keep hidden even in this rough country, so we made camp in the lower treeline of the foothills where we could plainly see the trail from the south, and anyone who might come near.

Buffalo Jacks wife Jill proved herself to be a most valuable member of the crew, along with her husband, they kept our bellies full. Jack's jokes and tall tales would keep everyone in happy spirits, which sometimes was not easy in territory one is unfamiliar with.

A friendship had grown between Jack and Mato Sapa, the black trapper that had joined us with Andre and Monty, back at the rendezvous. Mato Sapa, Long had told us, was Lakota for Black Bear, and so many of the men had just begun to call the man Bear. And a bear of a man he was too!

Bear was nearly six feet and six inches tall and probably weighed nearly three hundred pounds if not more. His face was scarred from many battles, and he had an intense look about him dressed in his buckskins and bear skin coat. With no hat to cover the long matted locks that fell from his head like tentacles of an octopus, Bear was an impressive man to look upon, if not quite a bit intimidating. Through Jack, we learned that Bears mother had been a slave, and had escaped her masters, and been adopted into the Lakota people, who welcomed her as one of their own.

Bear had become the primary hunter for our party by this time. He and Jill provided most of the fresh meat we ate. And the men had become accustomed to Jacks cooking, much to Tom's chagrin, they even liked his biscuits better than Tom's.

It was Bear who brought us the news that Long Walker was coming, and that he was not alone. He was coming into camp with a pair of antelope he had killed, and told us that he had seen two riders, two horses and one mule, a half a days ride to the south. He had never met Long Walker but his description was accurate enough that even though we came to readiness for a fight, I was sure this was Long Walker and Espinoza.

While we waited for them to arrive, Standing Fox who was our rear scout rode into camp and announced that he had seen a war party of Crow on our trail. At his guess about 3 days behind us. As well as a single set of tracks in the low country. In his report, "three horses, one white man, red hair."

"Now who do ya think that is?" Samuel mused. Then answered the question himself. "That no good Irish cousin o mine to be sure!"

"I wonder what he thinks he doing this far south, he should be well on his way to the Columbia by now, or St Louis." Tom voiced what I was thinking.

"I had a bad feeling I was going to have to deal with this thorn in my side for a while yet" I told them. "I could see the thirst for revenge in his eyes ever since rendezvous, he's out for blood now."

I took my spyglass out of my pack to scan the horizon to the north, but saw no sign of anyone in the immediate area. Something although did catch my eye. "Tom, here take this." I handed his the telescope and pointed, "About halfway up that knob there, just below the treeline. You see that?"

"Where?" Tom squinted through the glass while he answered "...about half way up which.. oh wait, are you talking about that.... what is that a coyote?"

"Too big for a coyote, maybe a wolf but I never seen one looks like that" I pointed out.

"Some kinda wild dog it seems, maybe a half breed wolf." Tom theorized.

"Yeah that what I thought too, look closer." I motioned for him to look again. "Its got the marks of a harness on it." I pointed out. "You see that too?"

"Ok wait now, you're right I think." Tom nodded as he handed back the spyglass, "What ya make of that?"

"I don't know. Maybe got loose from some tribe near here, they use dogs for travois here as well as horses, I saw a few at rendezvous." I told him.

"I think we have bigger fish to fry right now don't you?" Tom was always one to point out the more important thing in any given moment.

Bear, having over heard the conversation, broke in and said "I seen that dog a few times, over the last week or so, since we crossed the Ute pass trail. I think its following us cause it got left. Purty skinny too it is."

"Here they come, Silas" Cole pointed to the two riders approaching from the south. It was indeed Long Walker. And he had a Mexican with him who rode a mule.

Once they were dismounted and cared for their mounts we introduced ourselves. "My name is Silas Horn," I motioned to Tom, "This is my partner Tom Sweet." I extended my hand to shake, and he took it and introduced himself as Pedro Espinoza, and insisted we call him Pedro.

"Has Long Walker explained to you why we are in need of your help?" I asked him.

"Si Senior.. you have something you need to know the Spanish words on. It a letter?"

"Not exactly, we can talk about that later. First, you must be hungry and thirsty. You are welcome to eat and drink and we can talk later, when we are more alone."

"Gracias Senior. Gracias." Pedro nodded and followed Long Walker to the fire for some of the elk roast that was cooking there.

Once everyone in the party had got their fill of elk roast, beans, and sourdough bread, the men, as usual, went to their own fires, to smoke their pipes, or to pass the jug and tell their tall tales. It was at this time of day that everyone was relaxed, and lookouts were posted that Tom, Paul, Cole and I would make plans for the next few days. This evening though, I had been looking forward to for a long time.

Once all the men had filtered off on their own, Tom and I sat with Long Walker and Pedro and I brought out the map, or a piece of it, to show Pedro. I was not going to trust just anyone with knowing more than I wanted them to. I handed the portion of the map to Pedro, and eagerly waited while he read the side notes and markers.

After what seemed like more than a few minutes Tom spoke up and asked, "Is there a problem Senior?" To which Pedro only shook his head, and cleared his throat before he spoke.

"This map, is most certainly a copy of a map of the Conquistadore's Senior. The words are Proper Spanish, and not the Spanish that is spoken now. The notes are to show what the marks on the map mean, yet there are no names of places here that I recognize. The mountains I know, but not by these names."

"What do the notations indicate the markings are for?" I asked.

"Senior, how much do you trust the men you travel with?" He asked me, which surprised me for a moment.

"Well I trust them with my life or they would not be with me now." I answered him.

"I pray that you are correct" Pedro made the sign of the cross like the Catholics do before prayer. And bent his eyes again to the map.

"The markings read as so. 'traces of gold dust' which is marked with a star. The cross marks 'vein showing silver'. . ."

"Ok wait," I stopped him for a moment "Silver, Gold..." I looked at Tom before I continued, keeping my eyes locked on Toms as he also looked into mine.

"Go on Pedro." I motioned to continue while Tom and I both heard for the first time exactly what we were onto with this map. By the time Pedro was done telling us what the marks meant both Tom and I were in complete disbelief of what we had just heard. I had thought that perhaps this map would be helpful with our trapping and trading ventures with the local Indian tribes, who might be inclined to be friendly and who were more warlike. I was now confronted with a completely different reality

"Pedro, you said you came from a place called Taos. Is it located somewhere on this map?" Tom asked. Pedro nodded and pointed to a region at the southern tip of the mountain ranges.

"From what I can understand already of the mountains marked on this map," I pointed with the mouthpiece of my pipe "We are here, is that right?" Pedro nodded and agreed I had the right valley.

I reached into my possibles bag, and retrieved a gold twenty dollar coin and handed it to him over the map. When he took hold of it held it tight for a moment and he looked at me, "I will give you five of these, to guide us to your home, and show us some of these places shown on this map."

Pedro nodded, and when I released the coin, immediately tucked it away in this shoulder bag. "I must insist also that you tell no one of this conversation." I added, "And for that I will give you another one as well, once we return you to your home. Is this something you can do, Pedro?"

"Oh yes senior, for this amount I would guide you to Mexico City!" Pedro exclaimed.

Just then Tom brought up the idea that we needed more information of the surrounding country into which were going. The rest of that evening was spent learning of the Pueblo people, the Comanche and Kiowa, the Cheyenne and the Pawnee and others. All of whom were known to use the area for summer hunting grounds.

Pedro made specific mention of the Comanche being especially relentless in their raids on the local populations of Pueblo People and Mexican settlers in the area. "They are like demons, and kill with no remorse. They take their power from the terror they cause in everyone. They are not to be underestimated Senior."

By the end of the evening, and Pedro had retired for the night under a blanket by his mule, Tom and I both realized that our ideas on what we had come to do here, were now replaced with an entirely new reality. It was a long evening of quiet contemplation and hard thinking after that.

Chapter 17

Standing Fox and Bear crept up slowly, and silently through the damp underbrush, close to a camp where the fire shone bright in the night for anyone to see. They knew it to be the camp of David McNeil, who had been trailing our party for weeks now.

As they got close enough to hear voices, they stopped to listen and watch the camp and maybe find out more about what his plans were.

David, obviously drunk, was pacing by the big fire and having a conversation with someone who was unseen to them at the time.

"I'll get you cleaned up yet me boy, make ye a bit more presentable for the folks back home. You'll see, they are gonna give you the heroes welcome, I'll warrant it!"

The two watchers looked at each other, and back to the camp as David began to speak again, to no one.

"I know! Ye don't have to tell *me* how many men he's got with him. I was the one what counted them, you remember that now! You just relax and get your rest! You done your part already and now it's my turn to do all the work!"

Quite suddenly, David turned and ran to his pack, which sat half spilled open on the ground next to the poorly set tent, and reached in and pulled out a flour sack that was inside. "Ok, I got us a good fire goin' and some meat drippin' over it, you can come out now and get warm."

He sat on a big boulder nearby the fire and set the flour sack in his lap and stroked it to smooth out the wrinkles. "Won't do you no good to stay all cooped up in that pack all the time, you need fresh air, and a good warm fire!" He spoke to the sack as he slowly began to roll the edges of the sack from the top down.

As he rolled the sack down to his lap, the two watchers saw that is was a human skull in the sack. Which David began to stroke as if smoothing out the hair. "You are going to have to look your best for when I end the life of Silas Horn, so that he will plainly recognize you when I make your face the last thing he sees!" David peered in closely, picking an odd strand of hair that was left here and there, "I want to make sure he knows it was *us* who got our revenge at last!"

Finally satisfied with the appearance of the skull, he set it on a rock close by the fire, and reached to turn the pheasant he had roasting on the fire, which was already burnt on one side. David seemed to take no notice of this, and sat again on the boulder. He sat for a few minutes in silence, taking a few swigs off a whiskey jug. Then set it next to his brothers skull.

"Here ye go lad, drink up, ye earned it that ye did!" He looked intently at it, cocking his head to one side as if to hear better, then suddenly leaned back and almost fell off the rock on which he sat.

"Yes of course I have a plan me brudder, do ye think me daft?" He paused for a moment and pulled out his pipe and tobacco and began to load himself a smoke before he spoke again. "No of course I don't know where he's goin and neither, may I add, do you!"

While he lit his pipe with a tiny coal from the fire that he set on top of the tobacco, he began shaking his head, "Mm mm mm mmmm! No noo no no no no! That was *not* my fault! He wasn't alone he had that damn Indian with him! No no that would not have worked, I would have had the whole camp after me if I had done it then. I *knew* I should not ha' told ye about that!"

It was apparent to the two scouts watching, that this man had lost his mind.

David seemed to calm himself for a moment before he continued to speak. This time taking up his brothers skull and speaking directly to it. "No no me lad, I'll get him when he's alone, I'll make him tell me the secrets he keeps about that map, and then when he begs for his life I'll send him to hell! We can't be too hasty, and forget our priorities now can we?"

With his foot, he pulled the flat rock the skull had been sitting on further from the fire, and brushed off Michael's skull, then wiped it with a rag before replacing it on the rock.

"I think ill just gut him like what was done to you cause of him, and let him die the same way, while looking into your eyes!" David took out a long Arkansas toothpick and began to sharpen each side of the wide blade as he continued. "I even got *your* knife to do it with, that will complete the task nicely fer sure!"

Suddenly he jumped up and took out two pistols and cocked them, turning in circles he shouted "I know your out there I can hear you! You better not come any closer! I'll kill you, you hear me?? You done enough! *He's dead cant you see?? Leave him to rest in peace!*" He continued pacing around the fire, aiming his pistols into the darkness at random points as if some enemy was darting between the trees in the dark.

Standing Fox nudged Bear's elbow with his own and nodded it was time for them to retreat, nothing could be learned from one who had so clearly lost his mind.

"I'll kill you yet *SILAS HORN!!* You will see yet ya bastard!! You will pay for what ye done to me family! We will have *justice* fer Michael, I swear it!" He ran to the fire and dropped the two pistols, and taking up his brothers knife again, sliced the palm of his left hand deeply and watched the blood begin to flow.

"On the blood of me brudder, and me own, and that of my family and ancestors *I will have my revenge on Silas Horn! And you all here are witnesses!*" David swung the blade in a wide circle pointing at his invisible camp mates and the horses standing at the picket line oblivious. "You are witness to this vow! *YOU HEAR ME SILAS?? YOUR'E A DEAD MAN!*"

Chapter 18

"Well, if there was silver here, it was dug out long ago, or so deep in now we cant get to it." Tom said when we reached the end of the crude shaft dug into the mountain. "Looks like it had a cave in some time back so there may be, farther down."

I nodded in agreement in the flickering torch light. "This ain't too far in either, and this is hard rock. Would take a long time to dig a shaft like this for one man. I'd say if nothing else, we got a good idea now that the map is authentic. This is now the fifth site we've seen that was marked. It definitely led us to these spots and there is a shaft dug here."

I turned to go back to the entrance and Tom followed. "Id say Pedro was worth the money you're payin' him. He sure knows this valley." He commented as we came to the entrance.

As we stepped out into the bright daylight from the dark closeness of the shaft, the view that was spread out before us took my breath away for a moment. "Look at that would ya Tom? Ain't that about the most beautiful place you ever seen?"

The sun shone bright overhead, and showed every color of the land from the deep greens of the forests to the dark blue of a small lake situated in the upper end of the valley. Dotting the valley were the yellows and red, blues, purples and oranges of the wildflowers that grew among the thick tall grasses in the valley floor.

The northern end of the valley was encircled with steep bluffs and deep canyons that led down to the great gorge with the rushing river we had seen the week before as we crossed the pass to the east side of the mountains. The pass was just as Pedro had said it would be, though Long Walker had also confirmed before hand that it was the best and easiest way to cross the peaks in this area.

"Yeah its pretty, I suppose." Tom agreed.

"You suppose? Thomas look at this place!" I motioned over the land, "You don't see the absolute beauty of the Creator in all that?"

"I see a vast wilderness in which, at this moment in time, we are not welcome. That is what I see." he replied.

Just then Cole came up the steep incline from the camp below to tell us that Bear had come in from a scout to report the Crow were now crossing the pass we had come through just two days before. "They're getting closer Silas, and there's almost twice as many of them as us. We gotta find a place to fort up."

"Thank you Cole. We will be down shortly. Have the men get ready to mount up and move out." I told him. "I figure for sure they would give up the chase when we crossed into Cheyenne territory," I said to Tom "Guess I was wrong."

"Well we best find a place to hole up for a while, some good high spot maybe on one of these bluffs. Get the high ground on em." Tom suggested.

"No I think they're smarter than that" I shook my head, "all they have to do then is wait for us to run out of supplies.. or worse, water. I think we should get in those rocks there.." I pointed with one hand while handing him the spyglass. "There looks to be a good stream there that we can use if we need to hole up for a while."

"If we have to we can scoot out in any number of directions it seems, good cover too, in case of a fight. You're probably right." Tom pushed the spyglass shut and handed it back to me, "Never know, they may just push on past us if'n we're careful enough."

"One can hope." I said, "Let's go, Seems we got no more time to waste here."

"Might be best to backtrack a little.. and go back to where that dry wash is. It'll be best to leave as little tracks as possible showing our trail." Tom pointed out. This time I had to agree with him, despite the loss of time between us and the Crow, but in the end he was right and the time was worth being able to just disappear in a field of rock and shale. Once we had crossed that there would be no way for anyone to track where we had gone.

The next few days we spent camped out in a good defensible spot among the rocky canyons of the northers end of the valley. We made camp in a place surrounded almost entirely by big granite boulders the size of a modest home back in the east. In the middle of this, was approximately fifty to sixty acres of good grass for the horses, and a stream of good water flowing through one end.

Tom posted lookouts on the high rocks at the four directions, and Cole and the Indian scout Standing Fox took to exploring the area for possible escape routes, fallback positions, and places under cover with a good field of fire. The rest of the men set to building fortifications of stone and dead wood around the camps position which was backed up against an overhang from the bluff above.

Some of the places marked on the map were not far from our fortifications, so I looked around to see if I could find some of the closer ones. The terrain was steep, and rocky, but also beautiful in a twisted weathered kind of way.

One day when I got back to camp, Long Walker informed me that the Crow had gone on south and were now making camp among the Cottonwoods and Aspens of the foothills about thirty five miles to the south. It seems that they indeed missed our trail, but were not fooled for long, and were now most likely sending out scouts in all directions looking for us.

It seemed we were not going to be able to avoid a confrontation for much longer. So it was time to start getting the best of the situation, by choosing our own ground on which to make a stand. We might be discovered, but we would be discovered in a place of our own choosing, giving us the advantage. There might be forty fierce warriors looking for us, but we were nearly thirty in number ourselves, and forted up like we were, that would make each mans efforts doubled.

That evening, Jack and Jill had cooked up an antelope that Bear had brought in from his scout to the east. We had beans and rice, and some

Mexican flatbread Jill made that she called torteas. It was made with cornmeal, and cooked on a flat rock heated over the fire.

Over our meal Bear and Andre reported they had also found a route to the east from our position, skirting the high bluff through a steep canyon. Andre reported seeing buffalo as well as the antelope on the high plain the canyon opened up to at the other end. Through his gestures, interpreted by his partner Adam Forsythe, Monty the mute told us of seeing goats and sheep on the high cliffs that led down to the raging river below. The land certainly had a bounty of wildlife for such a rocky and seemingly barren landscape.

All in all we could go in any direction needed, with a minimum of danger given an ounce of care. I began to see the place in an all new light. A place like this could be a place to make a life.

According to the map, there were sulfur deposits and coal that could be used to make black powder. The bat caves being an acceptable source of the nitrogen needed for the explosive effect. As we had no source of saltpeter, the guano from the bat caves was the next best thing.

With those elements all within a few days ride, we would be able to make our own black powder and not have to rely on supplies from the east. This in itself was invaluable, but there was also one caved in shaft we had found already, that contained a good thick vein of lead, that with a bit of effort would provide us with nearly unlimited ammunition for our guns.

If even a small portion of the rest of the places marked on the map were also still showing traces of what the maps notes showed was there, this valley would be a very good choice for a man who had an adventurous spirit and an unending curiosity to make a home.

Chapter 19

One morning we all awoke to the smell of smoke. Not a thick choking sort of smoke. But a lingering taste of fire that permeated the air. The valley was covered in a bluish haze that indicated there was a grass fire somewhere to the south of us, and the wind was blowing it our direction.

"Ya think its them Crow?" Cole asked as we discussed possibilities, while Long Walker and the two other scouts went for higher ground to see what was the source of the haze.

"Could be lightning from that storm last night, put on a pretty show for a while there." Tom suggested.

"Any number of possibilities here," I said "And all of em are potentially bad for us."

Bear suggested we take the trail around the bluff, which would take us miles to the east, and see if we could discover the cause of the fire and its relative position to ours.

Long Walker came back about an hour after leaving, alone, and reported that from the high hill close to our position, only more haze could be seen. The other two scouts, Standing Fox and Andre LaFleur were circling another bluff for a better look, and would report back later.

"I think Bear is right," I told the men, "We need to get a better idea of whats going on, and we cant go far south or the Crow will surely find us. We cant go scouting with our full strength, so we will have to take the east trail, and find out exactly how much trouble we're in. If that fire is headed here, we have to know now!'

It took only half a day to reach the other side of the butte, and we saw no sign of a fire there, but could smell it in the air still, though more faintly here than at our camp.

We pressed onward south, and soon what was happening came into view. The valley floor had indeed been set afire, and though we could not see how, what we *could* see, was that there looked to be nearly a dozen people who had become trapped by the flames.

"Pueblos." Long Walker informed us.

"A number of them seemed to be injured, or so tired from runnin they jus give up." Bear said, as he looked through his own spyglass. "They gonna die, we don't help em." He added.

There was no debate or discussion, I gave Bolt a squeeze with my heels and we took off at a gallop for the trapped Indians.

The rest of the men, having the same thought as I, did the same, with no orders from me. It was going to be a delicate operation, as horses have a natural fear of fire, so this was going to be a good test of these new horses, and our training of them these last few weeks.

We circled the flanks of the fire, which was shaped in a half moon, with the tips being closer to the Indians than the center. The Indians had tried to climb the rocks of the bluff, but due to their burned feet, they were unable to climb, while the fire encircled them. When the Pueblos saw us coming, some began to yell, some screamed, and there were a number of children who were crying, but they still did not run.

"They injured" Bear shouted. "Look at they feet, they cant walk! They already burned!"

It took us a number of tries to get even one of them to trust us enough to help them, and that was only achieved when Bear tried the hand sign language known throughout the tribes, to tell them we wished to help.

Once they agreed, partially because the smoke becoming thicker in the air with the rapidly approaching fire, and partly because they had no other choice, we took all the children first as we could take two on each horse along with ourselves, and get them out of danger.

When we returned, there were several who were still hesitant , until I got down off Bolt, and lifted one of the older women onto his back and motioned to another close by to join her. The other men took this idea as well. We were going to have to run and it was going to be close, we had all had to use our scarves over our mouth and nose to keep from inhaling too much of the thick white smoke. The flames so hot and getting so close, as to start to burn and shrink the leather of my buckskins, as we ran for our lives leading our horses carrying the Indians out of the way of the fire.

The wind was indeed pushing this fire north towards our camp, and I had hopes that the wind would shift and change the fire's direction, but not full hope.

Once we got the Indians out of the way of the fire, and could asses their injuries, we could see they needed water first and foremost. We took them to a little stream to the east of the fire, and set them all by the water to bathe their wounds. The children still crying, and some still terrified of us in spite of the fact we had just saved them from a horrible death.

Long Walker explained after a hand sign discussion, that these people had never seen a white man before, and were therefore afraid that we would be like the Spanish that would enslave them, or the Comanche who would use them for sport.

It was in fact the Comanche that had set upon these Pueblos and tortured them and raped some of the women and killed some of the young men. Those they didn't kill outright, or take as captives, had had pine tar smeared on their feet which had been set ablaze by the Comanche, burning their feet extensively. Once they were done with their fun, they released the Pueblos that survived out onto the high desert, and set the grassland afire behind them.

Samuel took off his hat and wiped his brow, still coughing a little from the smoke, "Holy God in Heaven, Silas what the hell kinda place ya brought us into here?? I hadnae heard of anything like this since the stories my grand da used ta tell me of the Highland Wars back in Scotland! But that was a hundred years ago!"

"Pedro did say the Comanche were fierce, 'devils' he called them remember?" Tom broke in to say.

"The question is," Tom spoke up, "What do we do *now?* We cant take care of em, and we got to get back to camp and move it out or its gonna be gone time we get back."

"Long, ask these people if they have other nearby, that can be found to come help them, if so take them, you and Standing Fox, and get them some help." I had to think fast, because Tom was right, as usual. "The rest of us are gonna scoot back to the camp, and burn it before the fire does!"

"Did I hear ya right, Silas? Have ye gone daft man?" Samuel couldn't believe he heard me say that.

"Come on we got no time to waste, Ill explain on the ride back." I told him.

Once it was confirmed that these Pueblos had a village not far off, it was decided we would divide for now. Standing Fox and Long Walker, along with Andre and Bear, would see the Pueblos to their village, and Tom and I would go with Samuel and the others back to camp. If there was no camp to come back to later, we would meet on the back side of the butte, in the scrub pine and twisted hemlocks out of the way of the fire protected by the butte.

It would be nightfall before we got there. I just hoped we would get there before the fire did.

· · · ·

"WHO ARE THOSE? THEY are not Cheyenne, or Pawnee. Why would they care about these little people who have nothing?" Chasing Storm mused to his fellow Comanche as they sat on a high bluff to the south of the fire, to watch the scene unfold. "Who would bother to aid such a weak people?"

"White men, like the ones who take the south of Comancheria by Rio Grande." Short Wolf replied.

"White men." Chasing Storm had heard of these white men before. "Why the white men come here? There is nothing that does not belong to us!"

"They come because the Spanish are gone now. They claim it for themselves, without asking they come and take." Bloody Horse had had experience with whites in the south, in Texas, and knew this was not a good omen.

"They will not take from me!" Chasing Storm vowed, "I will take their hair and their livers, and cut their hearts out and burn them in our fires while they watch with dying eyes. Every one of them that comes!"

"They have taken much from us to the south, and their numbers are growing," Bloody Horse reminded him.

"They are few here, we will make them a marker of Comanche Territory, and leave their bodies to wither in the sun for all to see who come after them." Chasing Storm replied, then reigned his horse around to descend the butte, and track down these meddling whites in his land.

· · · ·

BUFFALO HEAD AND CRAWLING Dog, perched on a butte lookout rock, watched as the scene unfolded below them in the valley. The watched as the fire was started, and the Pueblo people set loose in front of it.

On a scouting trip for buffalo and elk, they had been in just the right place at just the right time to witness the entire series of events. The People had clearly been wounded and beaten so badly they had given up their spirit, and resigned to their deaths.

The Numunuu people would have to be tracked down, as obviously they were one of the more violent bands in the upper valley territory. It is one thing to raid warriors, and steal horses, but to torture people, to take them to sell as slaves, this must not be allowed to continue.

They were about to turn to go, return to their village and report to the Elders what they had seen, and something they had never seen before happened right in front of their eyes.

As the fire was about to completely trap the wounded people against the ricks off the bluff and engulf them, a party of strangers rode in and saved them from certain death. They were not Arapaho, Or Apsaalooke, they were not any of the tribes that came to these lands. They rode the spotted ponies from the Powder River people.

As they watched, the people were rescued after some obvious resistance, and taken a safe distance from the fire and their wounds tended to. The strangers gave them blankets, as they had been stripped of everything by the Nʉmʉnʉʉ. And it seemed they had someone who could speak to the Pueblos, even though they were strangers. It looked as if the strangers were going to help the Pueblos get back to their camp, as a good bit of hand signs and pointing was done before the party divided into two directions.

Once the party of strangers had split up, the two Cheyenne Warriors retreated back down the hill to their horses, and turned towards their camp to report this confusing scene.

Once the elders heard of this, much would need to be discussed so one could know what to do about it. The hunting camp of the People was not far, and the Elders needed to know that the Nʉmʉnʉʉ were again raiding this far north. In Buffalo Head's opinion, it was time to teach these little bands of raiding savages the lesson they had been taught in the time of their grandfathers. This is the land of the Tséhesenéstsestotse!! And this kind of rampant evil would not be tolerated here!!

Chapter 20

We rode into the night to get back to camp. I expected there to be smoke and chaos when we arrived, but I didn't expect the smoke to be black powder smoke, and the chaos to be a battle with the Crow!

We had rode straight into another fire! The fire of Indians shooting arrows of fire into the canyon trying to set the grasses alight and burn us out! I could see the flashes of the rifles of the men on the high rocks, who were keeping the party of attacking Crow at bay. Jack and Jill and a couple of the others were furiously trying to extinguish the fires that had started in out little fort, that would certainly spread and trap us in no time if not put out.

There was no time for discussion of battle plans, or strategy, there was a fight already happening. Tom and I rode to the front of the battle, and the others behind spread out to either help put out fires, or to defend a position that seemed to be under attack.

These men were all veterans of battles with the Indians, whether it was in the wars, or in the mountains trapping. Each man knew where he could be of the best use, and jumped straight into it!

When we reached the rocks that formed a sort of natural wall at the edge of our camp, we hunkered down with our rifles. Now and then we would see a flicker of light out in the field, right before a flaming arrow would come flying in our direction. Upon closer inspection, I noticed little glowing places all along the treeline on the other side of the little clearing. They were dug in for a knock down drag out fight.

We heard shots going off from around the edges of our little hideout valley, so the Indians were also trying sneak attacks on out border, looking for weaknesses. I think they knew better than to try to attack with a frontal assault on such a fortified position, but they were certainly coming.

Throughout the rest of the night, once in a while Samuel, Tom, Cole and I who were all holed up in the same set of rocks, thought we saw Indians creeping up on our position in the dark, as there was very little moonlight above the clouds. A time or two, one of us would take a shot at what we thought was an enemy, but never had any way to confirm it.

"What the hell we gonna do now Silas? They gonna come in hard when the sun comes up you that right??" Cole whispered. "We oughta use the dark to git on outta here! Go back out the way we just rode into this!"

"We *could* just skedaddle Silas," Samuel whispered. "Just may have to leave the trade goods cached away in that hole we found. Come back for it later."

It *was* a good idea, and I seriously considered it for a while. That is until Long Walker and Standing Fox rode in like their horses tails were on fire. Standing Fox with an arrow in his thigh, and Long Walker streaming blood from a gash on his forehead.

"The Comanche attacked us on the way back from the Pueblo village. Maybe twenty warriors, they followed us, but we lost them in the canyon I think." Long Walker reported. "We left Andre and two others to hold them at the narrow place in the rocks."

"Well, they just shut the back door!" Samuel whispered, "seems were fated to give our last here!"

"We been in worse spots than this, back in the war, but I don't remember when right now." Tom commented.

"Long, you injured? Can you fight?" I asked. To which he only nodded, and turned to go back to help the other plug the read entrance from attack.

It was a long night. Eventually the Crow stopped shooting fire into our perimeter, and it got eerily quiet. By this time those who had been putting out the little fires started by the arrows, had been successful and though on edge, everyone settled in for a long night of siege.

About the time the first grey light of morning began to show, the Indians put up a chorus of screams shouts and war cries, undoubtedly to put the fear of God into us, and we began to throw some lead their way in an effort to let them know we weren't going to just stand and die! We were ready for a fight!

All at once, through the mist of the early morning, we saw about twenty warriors charging across the field at full speed on their horses! It was a spectacular sight indeed! I had *always* been fascinated with the tactics the Indians used in war, as my father had taught me some of them back in the days he also taught me the intricacies of the fur trade.

They had no fear of our guns, they rode straight for us! Even when we were able to pick one or two off their horses as they got within range they still were not deterred! It was not until Tom was able to pick the leading warrior off his pony just before he breached the ring of rocks with his lance that they all turned as one, like a flock of birds, and retreated across the field. No doubt to regroup and pick up reserves for another attack.

"I hear shots from the canyon Silas, I hope them boys can hold em off, or were all dead!" Cole shouted.

"Well if they're comin' fer me, ill certainly take a few with me!" Samuel yelled from his position.

At this point Adam Forsythe ran up and threw himself into our firing position, out of breath, and reported through his panting, that Monte the mute and a couple others had decided they were going to skirt the bluff to the right of where we had forted up, and try to flank the Indians when it got light.

"Flank em? There's no way he can get around that bluff by now!" Tom pointed out. "Why the hell would he think that would help any at all??"

"No Sir," Adam corrected himself, "They goin *over it!*"

"Over it! But they'd have to be mountain goats to get over it by now!" Cole interjected.

"Or the next best thing." I said "The men who hunt them mountain goats! Ill jus bet they do it too!"

"You might be right after all." Tom agreed.

In that moment our conversation was interrupted by another ruckus the Indians were making across the field, and when we looked out to see which way they would attack from this time, we saw them charge, but they were charging at right angles towards a spot we couldn't see behind another hill to our south.

About this time we heard shots from the position to the right of the treeline that the Crow had been using for cover during the night. We then realized that Monte and his crew had begun his flanking maneuver from the rocks above the Indians encampment.

"Mount up Men!" I shouted "Were taking the fight to them! They're on the run now!!' And we mounted up and the dozen or so of us who were holding the front, now charged to the battle as Monte and his mates ran them off from the rocks above!

As we charged down the hillside and around the knoll to the south, we soon found out that these Crow were not retreating from *us* but in fact were now in a battle with *another Indian tribe!!*

These newcomers to this battle, far outnumbered the Crow, and between fighting the newcomers, and our attack from the rear. It was not long before there were only a few of the Crow that remained mounted, and at once they whirled around and took off for the hills to the north.

A few more of our men, along with Jack and Jill now had followed us out of the fort, leaving the rest to keep our rear protected, and rode up to where we now were faced with a whole *new* dilemma! *Who were these people and were we going to have to fight them too??*

It was a long tense moment before Bear rode up from the rear, and began to tell thank these newcomers for helping us fight off the Crow using prairie sign language. It was a short conversation, as they also knew that the Comanche had followed us into our canyon entrance, and told us they were enemies to the Comanche, and would be happy to help us rid ourselves of this problem as well. But they also told us that we were far outnumbered. And that It would be a hard fight, even since we have guns, as the Comanche have guns too!

This of course was disheartening to hear, it was indeed going to be a long tough fight if these warriors had guns.

The warriors in this party introduced themselves in some way I didn't recognize, and Bear, translating for us called them Cheyenne, which was a name some of us recognized. These were fierce and venerable warriors of the highest kind. It was only by luck that they had come upon our position while we were in the midst of a battle with the Crow.

A couple of their scouts had told them of us helping the Pueblos, and were on their way, they thought, to fight the rogue Comanche band committing these atrocities, when they rode up on the Crow instead. Also being intruders to the land these warriors claimed, the were to be run off for trespassing.

Once Bear explained the situation to me, translated from these Cheyenne, a plan came to mind. But we would have to implement it quickly, or we would be over run before we were able to pull it off.

I instructed Bear to invite these warriors into our camp. They were to be treated as guests, and discuss a plan that would indeed benefit both of our people's interests, with a temporary agreement between our two groups. They agreed, and we returned to the camp, where I sent everyone but Tom Samuel and I, to guard the rear, and keep the Comanche off our necks until we could mount an effective counter attack.

But it would take time, it would take patience, and was something that could not be *undone* once it was done.

Chapter 21

The leader of the Cheyenne, who's name translated to English was Battle Dog, sent his rear guard of ten warriors off to make sure no one could sneak up on us as we implemented our plan.

After some discussion of ethics with Tom, we decided ethics be damned we needed to survive the day, and this was the only way it could be done. The Comanche would eventually break through our defenses, as the Cheyenne told us they too were good in the mountains and no doubt would already be sending warriors over the butte, as well as those who were attacking the narrow pass in the canyon.

Cole, break out those Brown Bess's, we are gonna need more guns in this fight!"

Cole looked at me as if I were crazy, and inquired as to the wisdom of arming Indians we just met, and who just may decide to double cross us and kill us themselves. "How do we know that they wont just take the guns and ride off and leave us to fend for ourselves??" He also pointed out.

"I look in this mans eye," I told him, while I held the gaze of Battle Dog, knowing he would not understand my words, but would know my intention. "I look in his eye and I see honor and truth, I do not see an enemy. I see a brother." All the while Bear translated into hand sign. "If this man says he will fight with me, I will fight with him!"

When Bear finished his translation, Battle Dog nodded and made a few signs of his own, which Bear translated for Me.

"He says the Cheyenne will fight with the whites. The Comanche are invaders here, and they welcome the strangers to fight with them against the Comanche."

"Break em out Cole. Give em all a good supply of powder and ball too." I instructed. "Bear you teach them how to load and fire. Ill go help the men in the canyon, and you and the rest can get these warriors armed and ready to fight, and we'll hold em till you come.'

I left Tom and Samuel to help distribute the weapons and I rode into the canyon to help hold off the Comanche. By this time Monte and his men came in from their flanking maneuver and I took them with me to the rear. Men who could traverse the rocky and mountainous terrain as quickly as they had, were certainly of a great value to this fight indeed!

By the time we got to the narrows in the canyon, it was apparent that not only had our men plugged the canyon by dropping the first couple horses that had tried to ride through and attack, but they themselves had become pinned down among the rocks, and were barely able to hold off the warriors trying to encircle their position from the rocks above.

I looked to Monte to tell him to try to gain the high ground on the Comanche, but he was already motioning to his men that very same thing I was thinking. And they all disappeared into the rocks, while I distributed ammunition to the men defending the narrows.

The darkness comes early in these deep canyons, before actual nightfall, they take on a surreal feeling in the dusk like light of the early evening. Some tribes will not fight at night, and I was hoping that these were the type, like the Crow were, to hold a position during the night, and harass and taunt their enemies throughout the night to keep them on edge and wear on their nerves. If these Indians decided to attack at night there would be little we could do about it. It would be near morning before Tom and Bear and the men could arm and instruct the Cheyenne how to use the flintlock muskets, and then have them use them with any efficiency.

Fortunately for us, these warriors seemed to be so cocky, they would shout and whoop now and then, to distract us perhaps, from the rocks they would try to hurl down upon us from the heights above, while one of us would try to pick them off as soon as they showed themselves to do so.

As the night wore on, they tried to bounce bullets off the rocks into our position, and we would return fire, knowing we couldn't see to actually aim and hit anything, but then again, neither could the Comanche.

By the time morning came, there was a thick cloud of smoke wafting through the canyon towards us, that could only be a fire set at the mouth of the canyon in order to try to smoke us out of our positions, but we only covered our faces and continued to fire at any Indian we even *thought* we saw.

We had now been fighting one enemy or another for two days, and our strength was waning. We were not going to be able to hold out much longer, when just as the first rays of light dipped into the canyon, we heard the cries of battle in the rocks above, as well as behind us, as the Cheyenne joined in the battle armed with our Bess's.

Battle Dog had sent some of his warriors *over* the bluff, the same as the Comanche had done the day before, and now were engaging them in the heights above. As the battle progressed forward of our position, we also charged into the smoke to take the Comanche by surprise with a counter attack through their smoke screen.

When we got to the mouth of the canyon, the fight was on in earnest! Battle dog, unknown to me, had also sent warriors armed with our Bess's, around the butte to attack the Comanche from the rear, while the battle was joined in the rocks above, and at the mouth of the canyon.

The Comanche being armed only with old flintlock style muskets, were quickly overrun. And now we had *them* on the run!

Once we had turned the tide of the battle, and the Comanche were mounted and running south, the Cheyenne who had skirted the butte in the night gave chase, and we could breathe a little easier again.

We could still hear shots in the heights, but most likely were just the last few shots finishing off the now retreating enemies.

All around us we heard the war cries and victory shouts of the Cheyenne, a sound that gave me chills down my spine, and one I will remember for the rest of my life! We had survived two war parties! The Crow and the Comanche, and made a tentative alliance with the Cheyenne, all within a two day period!

The significance of this event didn't occur to me at the time, I was just happy to be alive and breathing still!

Chapter 22

We lost three men in the battle with the Comanche and the Crow, which while regrettable, seemed insignificant stacked against the odds *any* of us would survive! Once we had taken a couple of days to lick our wounds, and regroup, we were invited to the Cheyenne's hunting camp for a meeting with their elders. The warrior called Wakan Sapa had told Bear that they were interested in why a party of white men was in their territory, to which bear explained our intentions to make trade with the tribes. This seemed to be an accepted explanation as we were not only invited to come to their camp to meet their Elders, but we were encouraged to bring anything we had that we wanted to trade.

When Bear reminded them that they already had good guns of ours, and that we wished them to keep them as a gesture of good will, they began to relax their harsh persona's and the tension between two peoples who had just been forced into mortal combat with common enemies began to relax as well.

We spend about a week with the Cheyenne, in their summer camp, learning of their culture and their way of life. These were not only fierce warriors, but a people with a good collective soul. They only wished to live on the land of their ancestors and be at peace with their environment. Their warlike nature came from the generations long territorial disputes with other tribes, in which they were most often victorious, earning them a notorious reputation among all the tribes that frequented the area.

The one enemy that they feared and hated the most, was the Comanche, and their allies the Kiowa, that lived in the deserts stretching from the lower ranges of the rocky mountains, down into Mexico.

After a few days with the Cheyenne, Tom and I, being the "chiefs" of our party, were invited to a counsel with the Elders of the tribe.

They had discussed our presence in their territory at some length, and had agreed that since we had made enemies of their enemies the Comanche and Kiowa, that we were to be welcomed in Cheyenne territory as long as we conducted ourselves 'in a good way'.

Wakan Sapa, which Bear later told me was Cheyenne for Black Horse, presented me with an eagle feather, which Long Walker explained was an honorable gift indeed, and made it known that Wandering Dog and Head Hunter, the white warriors, would be considered brothers to the Cheyenne people, and as such, were to be treated as one of The Tsėhesenėstsestotse. The original People. The Cheyenne.

Bear told me that this was a great honor, to be accepted by the Cheyenne, in their sacred hunting lands. And that he was glad it was not *him* that had had such a great honor bestowed upon him, as it came with a great responsibility as well.

On Long Walkers advice, I chose a good breeding mare out of our Regatta of Appaloosas, as a gift to the warrior Battle Dog, who had made the split decision to help us fight the Comanche, as thanks for his wisdom in the moment, when many others would have just killed us outright, or left us to the Comanche to kill.

This deed came as a surprise to Battle Dog, who readily accepted my gift of thanks.

We made no mention of the muskets, and left it for the Cheyenne to understand that they were a gift from our people to theirs.

This was going to change our venture in this new territory immensely, as I had thought it would take a couple seasons of sporadic contact and trade in order to gain the trust of the people who lived here, but it seemed that the battle with the Crow and the Comanche had done that in a matter of hours.

It would take me a few weeks to understand the ramifications of this, but when I mentioned that I had found a place I wished to call home, I was told that as a Brother to the Cheyenne, I was already in my home, and that I was welcome to choose to stay or to go as I pleased. Which to me meant that maybe it *was* possible for me to pick a place in this beautiful, dangerous valley to call home!

Little did I know just how hard I would have to fight to be worthy of a place to live among these mountains and these people. I had been looking for a place to call home and to build a life. Away from fighting and war, away from the evil way people treat each other. But even though I was now welcome in such a wild and thrilling, beautiful and dangerous place, with the blessing and respect of the people who already live here, I would still have many battles to come, in order to be able to keep it.

www.ingramcontent.com/pod-product-compliance
Lightning Source LLC
Chambersburg PA
CBHW020533160726
47992CB00005BA/2360